A NIGHT AT THE SILK DUNGEON

Copyright © 2023 by M.L. Paige

All rights reserved.

The characters and events portrayed in this book are fictitious. Any similarity to real persons, living or dead, is coincidental and not intended by the author.

No part of this publication may be reproduced or transmitted in any form or by any means, electronic or mechanical, including photocopy, recording or any information storage and retrieval system, without permission in writing from the publisher.

ISBN 979-8-8726741-9-1

Printed in the United States of America

10 9 8 7 6 5 4 3 2 1

A NIGHT AT THE SILK DUNGEON

AN ASIAN FEMDOM NOVEL

M.L. PAIGE

ABOUT THIS NOVEL

This is a femdom novel featuring professional dominatrixes of Asian ethnicity. All interactions are consensual and all participants are 18 and older. A full list of kinks and fetishes can be found in the Kink Appendix section, though reading this list may spoil several scenes; a broad idea of what is not included in this novel is mentioned in the first chapter:

"Under no circumstances, will services rendered during the duration of the package include scarification, bloodletting, watersports, brown showers, or any permanent body modification, such as piercings, brands, or tattoos."

For select chapter considerations without reading the full appendix, see these potential TWs:

Several elements in Chapter 3 ("Business Time") and Chapter 4 ("Dinner and a Show") may prove intense for some readers, particularly around (separate) enema and feeding scenes. Additionally, Chapter 18 ("Pussy Whipped") contains elements of medium-hard whip play (with very little description of injury).

With that said, enjoy the story!

THE OMAKASE PACKAGE

By the age of 30, Preston Walton had established himself as an Ivy League grad, a software wunderkind, and one of the most desirable hires in all of Silicon Valley. By 40, he had been through three acquisitions, each earning him more money than the last, and five years after that he was leading software teams at one of the hottest companies in the Bay Area. He had staff meetings with some of the richest people in the world and spoke in front of crowds of thousands, but never had he been as nervous as he was now, sitting in Mistress Midori's office in the Silk Dungeon.

"Are you sure you want the Omakase Package?" Mistress Midori asked.

The Mistress was ten years younger than Preston, but in the warm lighting of the cozy reception office, dressed in an elegant, sleeveless emerald dress, she was the one with the gravitas, making Preston feel like a junior SWE on his first week at the job all over again. Her pale cherub face and blood-red lips seemed like a mask to him, one that never flinched or faltered.

"Yes," Preston said, his voice wavering.

Mistress Midori wrenched her lips to the side. "As you can imagine, I'm not in the business of denying clients what they want. But given that this is your first visit to the Silk Dungeon and your first experience with a BDSM provider, you can understand why I might want you to be certain that this is what you want."

The Mistress drummed her fingers on her lacquered, hardwood desk, pausing to consider her next question.

Finally, she asked: "Can you tell me *why* you're interested in the Omakase Package? We have plenty of packages popular with first-timers that might be a better introduction to what we do here."

Preston sighed, though he wasn't surprised. The Omakase Package was marketed as the Silk Dungeon's most premiere experience, an immersive, 24-hour visit involving the entirety of the Dungeon's Asian mistresses and fetish facilities. And while consent and safety were stressed as part of the experience, there was also a clandestine "anything goes" policy based on the results of a personality test that clients were required to take before beginning their visit.

Preston had already taken the three hundred question-long test and had eagerly and nervously been awaiting his meeting with Mistress Midori ever since. In a way, he felt like he'd been waiting for this meeting his entire life.

"I told you about my background," said Preston. "You know I've spent pretty much my entire life studying and working and pushing to get ahead. But the truth is… I'm 45 years old and I don't feel like I've really lived a single day in my life. I've always been drawn to kink stuff even though I've never explored it and don't take this the wrong way, but I've always been into Asian women too. You know, in a respectful way, not that cringey racist way."

Mistress Midori suppressed a smirk; perhaps she'd heard this kind of talk before.

"Anyway… I want to have an experience–an *adventure*–that makes up for lost time and that reveals something about myself that I can't get in a meeting room… or from some coddling first-timer's session. No offense."

Quirking a brow, Mistress Midori responded: "Like I said, I'm not one to deny clients. Well, not unless we're in a session." She laughed to herself. "We already have the rest of *your* visit all ready to go, in fact. But I do wonder if you're ready for it. A senior engineer working where you work–I'm going to guess it's been a while since you've truly not been in control."

"And that's what I want," Preston said, jumping in. "I don't want to be in control. I'm tired of being in control, so tired."

Mistress Midori slid an authorization form across the desk. "I need you to sign this if you want to continue. I suggest you read it carefully and not hesitate to ask me any questions."

Preston pulled the form towards him, scanning the block type. It was boilerplate CYA "cover your ass" legalese, the kind of thing you sign before going scuba diving or bungee jumping to acknowledge the risks and absolve the service provider–the Silk Dungeon, in this case–of responsibility should things not go as planned. At the bottom in bold was a line declaring the limits of the Omakase Package:

"Under no circumstances, will services rendered during the duration of the package include scarification, bloodletting, watersports, brown showers, or any permanent body modification, such as piercings, brands, or tattoos."

Below this supposed reassurance was a line for Preston to fill out the date of his last physical and to confirm that he had no known health issues that might need medical attention during the duration of the Omakase Package.

Preston looked up with a nervous laugh. "This is part of it, isn't it?" he asked. "A little bit of theater, like a warning label on the Blu-ray of a scary movie?"

Mistress Midori didn't return the laugh, not even to put Preston at ease. Her blood-red lips remained a passive flatline. "I would be more than happy to pivot you to one of our more popular starter packages, if you'd like. The Empress Package and the Lotus Experience are excellent and, I assure you, far from *coddling*."

One thing Preston's life of career success had taught him was this: Those who compromise never achieve anything great. He filled out the details of his last physical and signed the authorization form, sliding it back over to Mistress Midori.

"So, when do we begin?"

Mistress Midori took the form and placed it into the desk drawer, locking it after. She gave him a sad smile. "You seem like a sweet person, Preston. I really wish you'd reconsidered."

Preston fought back the urge to roll his eyes. This was getting to be a bit much. "I'm sure I'll–"

BANG BANG BANG! BANG BANG BANG!

Someone was pounding on the office door.

"I really am very sorry about this," Mistress Midori said. "Just understand, it's not personal. If I don't make an example out of you, the Silk Dungeon is going to become nothing but a playground for rich tech brats and I refuse to let that happen."

What the hell is she talking about? wondered Preston.

"Come in," the Mistress said glumly.

Preston turned as the door burst open. Two Asian women stood in the doorway, both not a day over 30. They wore what looked like dark navy police or prison guard uniforms that consisted of an officer's cap with a silver insignia, a fitted short-sleeve, button-down shirt and matching snug, hip-hugging pants with an oversized belt from which hung handcuffs, keys, and a few other inscrutable items. Before he could get a better look at the women, one was throwing a black nylon hood over his head.

"What are you doing!" shouted Preston.

He was pushed up out of his chair and slammed against Mistress Midori's desk, its edge catching him in the hip. He grunted in pain. He felt his arms pulled roughly behind his back and then there was the cold, icy kiss of metal around his wrists and the distinctive *click* of handcuffs being fastened.

"Up! Stand up!" a sharp female voice hissed.

Preston was forced to his feet, stumbling blindly as two sets of hands pushed him away from the desk.

"Are you sure about this, Midori?" asked another female voice, this one softer.

"It has to be done. He signed the form, we'll be fine. Try not to hurt him unless you have to," said Mistress Midori.

There was a derisive snort from the direction of the sharp-voiced woman. "We'll try," she said mockingly.

Preston was marched forward, out of the office, feeling like the ground was going to fall out from under him any second. The women kept a firm grip on his arms, their pace brisk and tough to match.

"What's going on? Wait wait… let me talk to Midori. Just give me–"

The women picked up their pace and Preston stumbled, nearly falling over. They turned a corner and then another and another, disorienting Preston.

"Slow down!" he demanded, feeling irritated and dizzy. "Please, I can't keep up with you with this thing on."

Someone smacked the back of his head in a decidedly unplayful way.

"Shut up," the sharp-voiced woman said.

A few minutes later, they stopped. Preston heard the jingle of keys and then a creaky metal door swing open. He was marched inside. The door slammed shut moments later and Preston felt the women's gloved hands searching his pockets for wallet and keys and other belongings. Once his pockets were emptied, he was pushed down onto an uncomfortable metal chair. His heart raced as he waited until finally the nylon hood was pulled off.

They were in a room with concrete floors and cinder block walls, outfitted only with a metal table, the chair Preston was sitting in, and two chairs on the other side. A bare bulb hung from the ceiling, casting sickly white light down on the metal table. As his eyes adjusted to the bright light, Preston looked at the two women who had so brusquely escorted him here.

The first thing Preston noticed was that the uniforms had nametags.

The one belonging to the woman on the left read, "M. Miss Ying." She was tall, with silky, straight black hair and the sort of long neck and ever-so-slightly harsh features that Preston associated with runway models. The bow of her pursed, matte red lips was crushed into a frown and her brows had been shaped into thin, placid arches, accentuating the subtle, red eyeshadow that gave her eyes a fashionable yet menacing look. She seemed lithe beneath her uniform, the belt cinched around an impossibly small waist for the tall Chinese woman.

To the right was her partner, whose nametag read, "M. Miss Grace." Maybe it was just the name, but right away Preston could tell this woman was Korean. While not as tall as her partner, she still had a strong, almost athletic frame with full hips and a heavy bust that stretched the tight fabric of her dark navy uniform. Long, honey-tea brown hair tumbled past her shoulders and down her back, its golden highlights a stark contrast to the woman's powdered-pale face with its pink blush and full, cherry-pink glossy lips tweaked into a suppressed smile. Thin eyeliner and long lashes made her eyes seem unnaturally large as she stared calmly at Preston.

"Do you like Asian pussy?" asked the woman on the left, Miss Ying.

"What?" asked a confused Preston.

Miss Ying slammed her gloved hand down on the metal table, startling Preston. "It's a simple question: Do you like Asian pussy?"

"Uh, I mean I, uh, you know—"

"Uh, uh, uh," said Miss Ying, mocking Preston's hesitation. "Are you fucking retarded or something?"

The woman on the right, Miss Grace, laughed. "Maybe he's got that engineer thing. Ass burgers or whatever."

"Are you an ass burger?" Miss Ying asked him.

Preston's first instinct was indeed an engineering one, to correct the women that the term they were looking for was *Asperger's* and that "retarded" was no longer politically correct. He somehow thought they wouldn't care either way and held his tongue.

"No, I don't have that," he said quietly.

"So you CAN speak," said an exasperated Miss Ying. "So can you please answer my fucking question already? Asian pussy, yea or nay?"

"Yea," said Preston, feeling a slight blush in his cheeks.

"I'm shocked," said Miss Grace with faux surprise. "A nerdy, white guy in tech who likes Asian girls. It's a world's first."

Miss Ying snorted a laugh. "So what's your body count? How many Asians have you fucked?" she asked.

Preston went quiet. His "body count" was just a measly three, four if getting to third base counted.

"It's not going to be a lot," Miss Grace said to Miss Ying matter-of-factly. "I mean, he's not ugly but those tech ass burger people don't exactly have a lot of game. I'm going to guess… seven."

"Seven? I bet this retard is a virgin," said Miss Ying.

Preston made a face, ready to defend himself.

"Look! He got angry at that!" shouted Miss Grace excitedly. "He's not a virgin."

"Well?" asked Miss Ying, looking at Preston, a snide smile spreading across her face.

He mumbled something neither woman could hear.

"Speak up," whined Miss Grace.

"Four," admitted Preston, deciding he would count third base after all.

Miss Grace looked disappointed. "Oh. That's… sad," she said.

"You're in your 40s and you've only fucked four people?" asked a bewildered Miss Ying.

"Wait, maybe he just means four Asian girls," offered Miss Grace. "Maybe he's fucked a lot of other people,"

The women looked at Preston but his expression said it all. They burst into laughter at the same time.

"Damn, that *is* sad," said Miss Ying. "I don't even wanna tell you my body count, it would just make you feel bad."

"Mine too," said Miss Grace.

As it was, Preston was beginning to feel plenty bad already. And even though he was eager to talk about something–*anything*–else, Miss Ying was far from done with the topic.

"But Miss Grace is going to make you feel better," said Miss Ying. "She's going to let you sniff her fine, Asian pussy. All you have to do is get under the table and it's yours. Isn't that right, Gracie?"

The voluptuous Korean girl nodded, flashing Preston a glossy smile. "That's right." He saw her spread her knees underneath the metal table. "Just come down and get a big sniff."

Preston hesitated.

"Unless you were lying about liking Asian pussy," said Miss Ying in a warning tone. "Bad things happen to liars here. Isn't that right as well, Gracie?"

Miss Grace gave an exaggerated nod, her heavy breasts jiggling slightly underneath her tight navy uniform blouse. "*Very* bad things," she said.

Not wanting to find out what the women meant—and not altogether put off by the prospect of putting his face between Miss Grace's legs—Preston clambered off his seat and awkwardly lowered himself to his knees so that he could duck below the table. As he inched towards Miss Grace, his head bonked the metal and one of the women laughed; Miss Ying, he thought. Miss Grace pointed a soft pink nail down at her crotch, guiding Preston in closer. Once he was close enough, she gently closed her legs around him so that the insides of her knees pressed against his shoulders.

"Now, take a big, big sniff," cooed Miss Grace.

He did as he was told.

As he breathed in through his nose, Preston smelled her earthy, woodsy vetiver perfume along with a musky hint of her sex. His cock stirred and he took in another inhalation, filling his lungs with the heady aroma while Miss Grace squeezed him between her strong legs.

"Keep breathing her in and listen to what I'm going to say next," ordered Miss Ying. "You are now our dog. You will obey our commands and do as you're told, no matter how scary they seem or sheepish you feel. Obey, and you will get treats, like this. Screw up or even worse—resist—and you will be disciplined, severely. Is that clear?"

"Yes," said Preston, feeling like he was speaking directly to Miss Grace's uniform-clad crotch.

"Yes, Miss Ying," Miss Ying corrected him.

"Yes, Miss Ying," Preston repeated back. His cock was poking hard against the front of his pants now as his head swam with Miss Grace's warm, sultry scent.

"Okay, that's enough sniffing for you, puppy," said Miss Ying. "Come on out."

Begrudgingly, Preston shuffled out from under the metal table, his cock tenting his slacks comically.

"Oooh, puppy's excited," taunted Miss Grace.

Miss Ying stood up, followed by her partner. They stepped around Preston and towards the door. Miss Ying swung it open and patted the outside of her hip.

"Come along," she said. "We have to change you into something more suitable of your… status here."

Preston went to stand and Miss Ying snapped her fingers angrily.

"You can stay on your knees," she said. And with that the women strode out of the room, leaving Preston to catch up.

GIVE A DOG A BONE

Preston rushed down the hallway after the uniform-clad women, knees thumping against the carpeted hallway. His body started to heat up from the exertion and sweat began to roll down his temples and along the back of his neck. The women didn't once turn back to look at him nor did they slow their gait, forcing Preston to struggle along in a shuffling, ready-to-fall-over motion, his breaths growing louder and more ragged the longer they went. All the while though, he was still hard under his slacks, still able to remember the slightest hint of Miss Grace's warm pussy.

Maybe this overnight visit–and whatever Mistress Midori seemed determined to do to him with the Omakase Package–wouldn't be so bad after all.

Miss Ying stopped at a painted, powder blue door with a big cartoony etching of a paw print on it. She threw it open and Preston looked inside. It was like a doggy daycare mixed with a kennel, all the furniture and equipment done up in bright blues and pinks. She waited with the door held open for Preston to anxiously shuffle inside, and once he was in, Miss Grace undid his handcuffs.

"Take off your clothes," she told him.

Preston wavered, still keenly aware of his hard-on. Then Miss Grace shot him a conspiratorial look before she glanced in Miss Ying's direction, as if warning him how he might anger the other woman should he not do as she commanded. Sheepishly, Preston took off his button down and undershirt, and then his shoes and socks and slacks, leaving him just in a pair of boxer briefs.

"Those too," muttered Miss Ying. "Dogs don't wear clothes."

With a small sigh, Preston pulled off his boxer briefs, revealing his still hard cock. He looked down, trying to make eye contact with the young Asian women.

"Get on all fours," cooed Miss Grace.

Miss Ying was already retrieving some items from a high, white cabinet with frosted glass panels as Miss Grace went around behind Preston and reached between his legs, causing him to jump as her gloved hand touched his cock. She drew her fingers down his shaft and then cradled his balls in her hand, the smooth leather of her glove caressing them. Preston gave a small, heated sigh.

"Puppy has *big* balls," Miss Grace said admiringly. Her words made Preston's cock throb.

"Oh?" asked Miss Ying, still collecting items from the cabinet. "Too big? Do you think he needs to be clipped?"

"Maybe," said Miss Grace. She hefted him in her palm as if weighing Preston's balls. "Puppies with big balls get into trouble. Are you going to get into trouble, puppy?"

"No, Miss Grace," said Preston, cheeks burning with lusty embarrassment at being talked to this way.

"We'll see," she said, not sounding so sure. "First we have to figure out if you can behave."

She let go of his balls. Miss Ying came over and dropped a small pile of bondage gear and other toys Preston couldn't make out at his side and the two women got to work. They pulled Preston's hands into black leather mitten sacks, cinching and belting them once his hands had been forced into tightly balled fists. They then slotted snug kneepads up each leg and put ankle cuffs on him before putting a leather belt around his waist to which they attached long snap hooks. As the women bent each of Preston's feet up towards his ass, he realized the snap hooks were meant to clip onto the ankle cuffs, making him after to balance on his knees. Thankfully the kneepads helped to take pressure off the awkward position, but between his leather mittened hands and his knees, Preston struggled to hold his balance.

They weren't done yet though.

Next, Miss Grace showed him a leather hood with little triangle doggy ears and a heavy duty zipper across the mouth, the only openings being for his eyes and two little slits for his nostrils. It took both Miss Ying and Miss Grace working together to pull the snug hood over Preston's face and even before it was on all the way he could feel how warm and constricting the heavy leather was. The women adjusted the hood, fastening its collar around Preston's neck. He noticed that the eye cut-outs caused his vision to tunnel slightly, forcing Preston to have to turn his head to the side to see his periphery.

Then she held up something that looked like a thin chain leash with a leather handle on one end and a strange-looking C-shaped piece with a small tightening screw on the other. She took the C-piece and got in close to Preston, guiding its ends towards his nostrils through the slits in the leather hood.

"This might hurt a little," she said as she turned the tightening screw.

Preston flinched as he felt the effect of the C-piece being tightening, its rounded but nevertheless steel prongs dug into his septum, making it so that when Miss Grace tugged on the thin chain leash there was a nasty pull on Preston's nose. He cursed through the gag in pain, his protests muffled.

"Too tight?" Miss Grace asked.

He realized she wasn't asking him, but Miss Ying.

"It's supposed to be tight," said Miss Ying. She crouched down and gave the chain leash a firm tug and Preston grunted in agony, the C-piece–a hook of sorts, he now realized–yanking sharply against the delicate skin on the inside of his nose. She looked coolly at Preston. "We're going to see how good your doggy skills are. And the *most* important doggy skill is being able to heel."

Miss Ying stood up, with the leash's leather grip in hand. She adjusted her stance so that the back of her tall officer's boot was no more than a foot away from Preston's hooded face. She took a step forward, the slack in the chain leash disappearing as it was pulled tighter, threatening to yank Preston's nose along with it.

"Heel, puppy," said Miss Ying nonchalantly, her stride lengthening.

In a panic, Preston crawled forward, wobbling on his knees and struggling to use his balled, mittened fists for balance. Miss Ying took another, longer step and Preston had to take a dozen little steps with his hands and knees to keep up. He felt his cock swing wildly and his balls slap up against the insides of his thighs, dimly aware how exposed he was to Miss Grace as she stood beyond him, watching his body flex and clench to try to stay in control.

Miss Ying walked Preston in a slow, unceasing circuit around the doggy play area, until his body was trembling and covered in sweat. The heavy leather hood didn't help. No matter how much he thought he had finally gotten the hang of the awkward dog-walk though, he would soon feel the nasty biting pull of the nose leash, grunting and grumbling under his zippered mask. And as she led him, Miss Ying continued to her commanding chant every few moments, going: "Heel. Heel. Heel." Miss

Grace took more of a commentator's role.

"Oooh, look at puppy go! Maybe he's been a bitch on a leash before. Have you, puppy? Is that why those balls are so big, because you've been spending so much time on a leash heeling instead of humping female doggies? Do you wish Miss Ying would let you hump her? I don't know, puppy, she doesn't seem like that kind of girl to me, but maybe if you're very, *very* good and you do exactly what she says, she'll let you hump her nice shiny boots. Wouldn't that be nice? Grunting away between Miss Ying's calves until you drain those big doggy balls dry?"

Aside from the obvious humiliation of Miss Grace's words, they had another effect on Preston–they made him *excited*, his cock staying rock hard as he painstakingly shambled after Miss Ying, his arousal dampening the pain from the C-hook in his nose. Miss Ying led Preston to the middle of the room, where Miss Grace was seated on a painted white stool. She handed the chain leash to Miss Grace and looked down at Preston with a cold smile.

"Very good, puppy. I think you deserve a treat," she said.

She disappeared from Preston's tunneled view. When she returned, he saw she had a small bottle of lube and a big, bulbous butt plug with a curly silicone tail jutting from its base. His eyes widened in fear.

"Every puppy needs a tail," said Miss Ying, smirking. "And you just earned yours."

Miss Grace reached out to scritch Preston's neck through his leather dog hood. "Head down, puppy," she said. "And ass up." Resting her hand on the top of Preston's head, she pushed him down, exposing his ass.

Miss Ying's heels clacked on the floor as she stepped around behind him. Preston heard the click of the lube bottle's cap and then felt the cool squirt of the lubricant as it rained down between his ass cheeks. There was a lot of it–not that Preston was complaining–and it ran down the underside of his balls and along the backs of his thighs. Preston whimpered in fearful anticipation.

"Awwh, don't worry, puppy," Miss Grace said, bending forward to speak to him in a hushed voice. "You'll feel better once you have a nice big tail filling you up."

As she did the words, Preston felt Miss Ying push the plug into him, his tight, puckered rim fighting the plug's unyielding girth. He groaned and his body tensed. There was no way the plug was getting inside him–it was too big. It seemed to grow larger and larger in Preston's mind as Miss Ying kept the pressure on, from egg-shaped to lemon-sized to the entire fat heft of a football. His groans became petulant whimpers as he tried to ward off Miss Ying's insistence by making her feel bad. The Asian mistress was not deterred.

"You're getting your tail one way or another," said Miss Ying. "So stop fighting it. Open up that ass."

Miss Grace whispered to Preston: "Just take deep breaths, puppy. Let it in."

Preston did his best. He forced himself to suck in long inhalations through the slits in his heavy leather hood and, as he let them out, he felt his asshole relaxing–almost the same way as when he relieved himself. He focused on that humiliating sensation and the plug slid in deeper; it was like it was pushing open his rim even more forcefully now, making Preston take longer, shakier breaths to calm himself. The only consolation were Miss Grace's fingers stroking his head through the dog hood, her hands idly playing along the leather-clad curve of his head. The long breaths he took drew in her scent tinged with the hood's thick leather smell and the effect was mildly intoxicating, making his entire body feel warm.

The plug reached a point where Preston thought it would tear him open. He tensed in panic.

"Almost there," whispered Miss Grace. "Take the deepest breath yet and let it out in a long stream…"

His body starting to tremble, Preston did as she said, his lungs filling as much as they could. He let the breath out and as he did there was a moment of shock as the thickest part of the plug pushed into him, making Preston see white for a split second. Then the startling sensation was gone and the plug nestled deep into him, his hole tightening around the plug's slender base. He took several ragged breaths while Miss Grace unscrewed the C-hook from Preston's nose and lifted him back to all fours; the silicone tail curling out from the butt plug jiggled back and forth.

"Wag that tail, puppy," ordered Miss Ying.

Grateful that he had the hood on to hide his embarrassment, Preston shook his ass and the women burst into laughter that was not altogether kind.

"White guys really don't have rhythm, huh?" asked Miss Ying.

Miss Grace covered her mouth as she laughed, shaking her head in agreement. She stood up and moved towards the edge of the play space, beckoning Preston to crawl towards.

"Over here, puppy!" she called, lightly slapping her full thighs.

Preston lumbered towards her awkwardly, wobbling back and forth with his "tail" bouncing everywhere. Its bulbous shape pushed against him from the inside and made his cock feel even stiffer, and as he excitedly made his way to Miss Grace he felt his cockhead slap against his bare belly, Miss Grace cooing patronizing praise the whole while:

"Come on! Over here, boy! You can do it!"

Miss Ying snickered. "I think puppy's got a crush," she said as Preston made it over to Miss Grace, his eager efforts rewarded by the Korean girl squatting down and drawing his head between her warm thighs. He sniffed at her crotch and she didn't stop him–in fact, she pulled him in even deeper, letting him take in the musky scent of her sex. He could feel the push of her pussy lips through the uniform and ached to feel even more of her.

"Is that true?" Miss Grace asked playfully, pulling Preston back to look down at his hooded face. "Bark for me if it's true."

His horniness overwhelming him, Preston–to his surprise–barked. "Woof! Woof woof!"

"Awwh, isn't that sweet," said Miss Ying mockingly.

"Yeah, so sweet," said Miss Grace, stroking Preston's cheek through the mask. "But you know you can never have me, right puppy?"

Preston whined, the sound half him playing into their roleplay and half hoping he might somehow be able to win this young 20-something woman over. Even though he'd made enough by that point in his life to get dates with women of Miss Grace's caliber, this was different. This wasn't a woman going out with him to get close to his money or even a hired sex worker–not that Preston had ever done that, though he'd thought about it from time to time. No, this was a woman who held *herself* over *him*, who despite her cooing, playful behavior, made him feel as if really *were* no more than an excited puppy to her. The abject power dynamics were thrilling to Preston and the more he thought about how unattainable Miss Grace was, the more he wanted her.

Miss Grace gave him an achingly beautiful smile. "Don't be sad," she said softly. She unzipped the mouth of Preston's hood and then slipped her fingers under the waistband of her pants, reaching down to her pussy. When she pulled her fingers out, they were slightly wet and glistening. She held them out to Preston. "Lick," she said.

Preston tongue lashed out, licking Miss Grace's wetness off her fingertips.

It was sweet and musky and he licked until her fingers were spit-slicked. She closed the zipper of his hood again and from behind, Preston heard the jingle of another chain leash. This one was much heavier and thicker than the one that had been attached to his nose and he felt as Miss Ying clipped it to a ring gaining of the collar of his leather dog hood.

"Time for a walk," Miss Ying said, pulling Preston away from Miss Grace. She stayed behind, waving to him as the tall, Chinese mistress led him back into the hallway.

BUSINESS TIME

Miss Ying walked through the hallway like she was marching down a fashion runway, forcing Preston to work hard to keep heeled to her boot. He looked up at the lithe woman, body shifting from side to side in her fitted uniform, wondering where they were going. Preston didn't have to wait for long.

They entered a narrow archway with a bend at the end of it, which opened onto a small expanse of fake grass. The walls were painted sky blue, with a bright orange sun hanging high up on the wall. Miss Ying attached the other end of Preston's leash to a metal pole sticking up out of the fake grass.

"Wait here," she said.

She disappeared for a brief moment and returned with what looked like an IV bag with a long plastic tube hanging from it and a small rounded rubber tip at the end. Miss Ying attached the bag to the top of the pole and with nonchalant, perfunctory movements, came around behind Preston and lightly grabbed the base of the butt plug wedged deep inside him.

"Take a breath," she said with none of Miss Grace's warm encouragement.

Realizing that Miss Ying intended to remove the plug, Preston took a deep breath in and then breathed out as Miss Ying pried the plug out of him; thankfully it was a lot less painful coming out than going in, although there was that now signature moment of shock as its girthiest part spread him wide.

"Don't worry, it'll be easier when I put it back in," she said.

It was hardly reassuring to think Preston wasn't done with the plug, but compared to what came next it was hardly a trifle. Miss Ying took the small rounded rubber tip hanging from the plastic tube and pushed it into Preston's asshole. He jumped, but his hole was already so loosened up that there was no resistance–the tip went in easily. Miss Ying reached up to the hanging bag and fiddled with a small valve, causing clear liquid to run down the length of the plastic tubing and into Preston, filling him with the cool, mystery solution.

It clicked into place then: She was giving him an enema.

"It's important to make sure your dog does his business when he's supposed to," said Miss Ying as she stared down at him, her harsh features tightening into a condescending scowl. "And since you aren't housebroken, we have to do this."

The bag continued to empty into Preston. At first it was merely just a little of the cool liquid, but as Miss Ying continued to squeeze out the contents of the bag through the tubing, Preston felt his ass being filled with more and more of the enema solution, until it started to feel as if he could take no more. He glanced up at the bag anxiously. It was only about halfway done. Preston whimpered, his insides becoming cramped, but Miss Ying ignored his noises and his squirming, working with the ruthless efficiency of a night nurse. Preston tried to distract himself by wondering if she'd once worked such a job, and then by thinking what kinds of work prepared someone to be a mistress in a place like the Silk Dungeon.

A nurse? Perhaps, with their distanced familiarity with the human body. Or maybe a salesperson, practiced in influence and getting what they want, or a teacher or hell, even a real police or corrections officer, someone to whom authority comes naturally and who is able to present their control over others as beneficial instead of subjugating.

Miss Ying squeezed the last of the bag into Preston. He could barely stand it now. She pulled out the rubber tip from his ass and discarded the enema bag and tubing into a discrete bin on the other side of the fake grass. Then Miss Ying pulled over a short seat, looking especially tall in it as she monitored Preston with icy indifference. He broke out in a sweat, feeling his stomach roil.

"You have five minutes," said Miss Ying. "Then I'll let you evacuate."

Five minutes?! Preston wasn't sure he could go another fifteen seconds, let alone five minutes. The idea of her "letting him" void his bowels was a very special kind of humiliation, the sort where his bodily autonomy was stripped away and placed in the hands of this callous yet beautiful stranger. She tapped her boot against the floor in a too-quick rhythm that made Preston antsy and unable to focus. He grumbled through his mask.

"Is there a problem, puppy?" she taunted.

Preston sighed through his nose and squeezed his bound fists to a slower rhythm than Miss Ying's boot taps, trying to project his thoughts anywhere else but being forced to hold in a quart of liquid inside himself. He grunted quietly, unable to help it, his body squirming and writhing like he was fighting off the fiery itch of sunburn.

"When I allow you to release," said Miss Ying, stressing the word 'allow' with relish. "You will hold onto the pole and move to a squatting position as best you can. You will look me in the eyes as you do so. Is that understood?"

It hit Preston then that he'd have to let this enema out *in front of* this modelesque Chinese dominatrix. He couldn't think of anything more utterly embarrassing than that. Well, he guessed he could–he was going to have to look her in the eyes as he did it.

"Is that understood?" repeated Miss Ying in her severe warning tone.

Preston couldn't bring himself to even try a bark and simply nodded his head, wondering how much longer he had to go. Surely they were in the final minute by now.

"Halfway there," said Miss Ying.

Only halfway?! How could that be? He grunted a sigh out and tensed and untensed his body, fighting to control himself. His squirming became more exaggerated and he started slightly rocking back and forth, stopping when he realized how the motion made him feel the sloshing in his bowels.

"You might not believe it, but I've always liked training dogs. Puppies like you especially," Miss Ying said with pride. "A lot of people spoil their dogs, coddling them with attention and letting them do whatever they want because it's cute. My approach is different. I think you need to have a firm hand to establish dominance, so that your dog knows who to listen to. My puppies might not have as much fun as others, but they wind up very, very obedient. I can promise you that."

She looked at the small wristwatch she had on.

"Thirty seconds. Do you remember what to do?" she asked.

Preston nodded again, desperate for the seconds to tick down. He wondered if he'd be able to get into the position she asked before his body gave in. He would have to do his best–he didn't want to imagine the alternative, not with someone like Miss Ying who seemed to get off on wielding her authority.

"Ten seconds," she informed him. "Five. Four. Three. Two… go ahead."

Preston grabbed the pole as best he could with his mittened fists, rocking himself back onto his feet in a dangerous motion that almost sent him sprawling onto his back. The horror of that near-calamity sent a shot of adrenaline through him and he righted himself, quickly getting into position so that he was on the balls of his feet, his weight making the stretch in his folded back legs especially harsh. His eyes found Miss Ying's dark, glassy stare and he released.

It was the single most humiliating moment of his life.

Along with the quart of liquid, a torrent of unmentionable awfulness came out of Preston in an uncontrolled gush. Miss Ying didn't make a face or even show the slightest hint of shock, which made it all the worse as she watched him calmly, making sure he didn't get to so much as blink as he voided himself in front of the statuesque Asian woman. Every time Preston thought he was done, there was a little bit more, until finally there was just a dehumanizing dribble of enema liquid leaking out of him.

"Are you done, puppy?" Miss Ying asked him with a cruel smile in her voice.

Preston nodded.

"Dogs don't nod. They bark. Are you done?"

"Woof," Preston barked, sounding dejected.

Miss Ying stood and grabbed a hose off the wall. The water from it was ice cold and Preston shrieked under his gag as she washed him off, clearing away his mess into some hidden runoff channel. She was thorough, making sure to get every last speck off him.

"Do you have to pee too?" Miss Ying asked. "If you do, you better do it now–if you have an accident later, I'm going to rub your nose in it."

Preston forced himself to pee, remaining in the uncomfortable squatting position as he arced out a stream of urine. Miss Ying sprayed him down with cold water after that too, Preston whimpering as the water rained down between his legs. Finally, when he was finished and Miss Ying had cleaned him down, she helped him get back into an all fours position off of the fake grass.

"Now to put your tail back in," she said.

Getting the plug back inside of Preston was a much different affair than the first time. Not only was his ass stretched out, but the grinding shame of relieving himself in front of the mistress made him accept the thick plug so much more easily, as if the idea of fighting against it or being embarrassed to expose himself was a distant, quaint concern. Miss Ying cleaned off her hands and gathered up Preston's leash.

"Good job, puppy," she said. "I have to use the bathroom too though."

At first, Preston assumed that Miss Ying would attach his leash to the metal pole and make him wait while she went off to the bathroom. But to his confused surprise, she had him follow her all the way there, making him wait inside the opulent, albeit cramped, bathroom while she attended to her own needs. Unlike with Preston, he was left facing away from the toilet, looking at the white tile wall as he listened to Miss Ying relieve herself. Somehow, Preston still felt embarrassed by this–and not for Miss Ying either, but for himself. Maybe it was how nonchalant she was about it all, how there was no shame or hesitation on her part, as if Preston really was nothing but a puppy on a leash who was forced to sit there and wait while his master–this mistress–made herself comfortable again.

He heard her flush and zip up her uniform before washing her hands. Then she tugged him back towards her and saw she was smirking down at him.

"You're lucky you know," she said to him in a low, sultry voice. "I've made unruly puppies come in here with me and make sure I'm clean after I'm done. Oh, I always am, but they don't know that, especially since I snap a blindfold over their eyes first. Imagine that–being told to lick someone's ass clean after they just used the toilet, sticking your face into that warm, fragrant, intimate place, not knowing what your tongue might touch…"

Preston was mortified as his cock stiffened, rising up between his legs. Miss Ying noticed it and laughed to herself.

"Then again maybe you're not so lucky," she offered. "Maybe you would've liked that."

Miss Ying's hands flirted with the button of her pants, undoing it as she slowly drew the zipper down. She shimmied the dark navy pressed slacks down her hips, revealing lacey black underwear underneath. Then she turned around and inched the lace down the smooth, pale curve of her taut ass. With a ballerina's grace, she bent forward, her ass cheeks parting ever so slightly.

"You're going to stay right there, puppy," she told him. "You are *not* allowed to put your face in my ass."

And just like that, Preston wanted to do it. His cock throbbed desperately and he took in a stealthy whiff of the mistress's musk, both ashamed and intrigued by what he was doing. Miss Ying let her ass gently sway back and forth.

"Your brain must be wired differently to come here and subject yourself to this," Miss Ying said in that husky, low tone of hers. "Most men wouldn't be able to control themselves seeing a woman so up close like this. They'd be trying to get themselves inside of her, wanting to take her–*fuck* her. But not you, right Mr. I've-only-fucked-four-girls? You're different. Maybe you only guessed it before, but now you're sure."

Miss Ying pushed her hips back so her ass brushed against the leather of Preston's hood and the zipper covering his mouth. He pushed his tongue helplessly against that zipper, wishing he could reach through and touch her, taste her. Miss Ying pulled her hips away again and brusquely pulled up her panties, tugging her uniform shirt back in and righting her look once more. She spun around with a secretive grin.

"Okay, I'm all ready to go," she announced. "And by now Miss Grace should have the girls ready for you."

The girls? Preston tilted his head to the side, trying to puzzle out what that meant.

"Oh, did we forget to mention?" Miss Ying asked, acting aloof. "The Silk Dungeon runs sessions for young Asian women looking to be more assertive. You know, nothing fancy, just a bunch of college girls and young professionals. And today you're the guest of honor." Miss Ying paused for a mischievous moment and then added: "Who knows, maybe you'll see some familiar faces."

Preston was all nerves as he followed numbly behind Miss Ying. Familiar faces? Young professionals? In his tech world, there were many, many homely male engineers but there was also a contingent of shockingly gorgeous, smart and savvy Asian women, especially those coming right out of college. Would Preston recognize anyone he knew?

Or perhaps more terrifying: Would Mistress Midori and the Silk Dungeon purposefully have sought them out for Preston's Omakase Package?

They reunited with Miss Grace at an elevator at the far end of the Dungeon, where a frosted over window showed that the day was inching into night. Preston had already been here for a few hours, though he barely felt hungry or thirsty in that time, his wonder and adrenaline too through the roof to think of small details like that. But now that he saw the darkening San Francisco sky, he felt his stomach give a slight rumble.

"Are they ready?" Miss Ying asked Miss Grace.

"Yep!" she said cheerfully. "They're upstairs having dinner."

The mention of dinner only made Preston more hungry. He looked at Miss Grace pitifully.

"Don't worry, puppy," she said to him. "We have a special meal for you, too."

Miss Grace rang for the elevator and Miss Ying led him inside. On his hands and knees, with the voluptuous, bubbly Korean woman to one side and the svelte, domineering Chinese woman to the other, Preston dreadfully awaited what was in store for him.

DINNER AND A SHOW

Preston did not expect the elevator to open on a private dining room with 360-windows that overlooked the city below. There were a half-dozen circular tables set up in a horseshoe around a raised stage, and at each table there were between five and six women, all of them well-dressed Asian women who were eagerly involved in raucous chit chat and snacking up until the moment the elevator doors opened. As the women started to notice the mistresses–and Preston between them–they slowly quieted, all heads turning towards the man-turned-dog at the end of the chain leash. A low buzz spread across the tables.

"They've been eager to meet you, puppy," Miss Grace said, taking the leash from Miss Ying. "Let's go say hi."

Introductions were dizzying. Preston was led from table to table, barely able to make contact with the stylish, attractive Asian women seated there. All things considered, the group was diverse–there were fairer-skinned East Asians, with twee, chichi fashion sensibilities; tawnier Southeast Asians who bore a more eclectic style, street style; and a scattering of what Preston thought were Central Asian or maybe mixed race women with uncanny looks that seemed to shift depending on the angle they turned. The women themselves were diverse too–some slender, some larger, some small, some tall.

Preston was made to go around to each and every one of them so that they could get a good look at the man in the dog-hood with his bound hands and folded back, kneepad-clad legs. More than a few of them were especially interested in his bouncing silicone tail and the unabashed sight of his cock and balls. One, a curvy half-Asian, half-white woman with a dewy face and gently parted lips, even asked to touch him and it took Preston a second to realize she wasn't asking him, she was asking the woman holding his leash.

"Sure," said Miss Grace encouragingly.

The half-Asian fondled Preston's balls and expertly grabbed his cock, showing no hesitation as she squeezed him in her hand.

"Who is he?" she asked Miss Grace. "You know, out there, in the real world. Someone important?"

Miss Grace hmmed. "Someone not used to being on a leash," she said.

"Well, I think he looks good at the end of a leash," the half-Asian said, letting go of Preston's cock to smugly pat his ass. Her light brown eyes bored into him. "This is wild," she said to herself and to the others at the table. "This guy is probably, like, 50 and rich and he's taking orders from a bunch of Gen Z girls. Wild."

When they were finally done with introductions, Miss Grace brought Preston on stage, where there were two tufted chestnut-hued leather armchairs and a well-worn doggy bed set between them. Miss Grace had Preston sit down on the bed and light laughter spread throughout the crowd. She joined Miss Ying, who was already seated.

"Thanks for coming, everyone!" said Miss Grace. "We're so excited to have you all here with us. As you can see, we have a special guest. Puppy, introduce yourself."

Miss Grace gave Preston a glossy-lipped smile, her stare urging him on. She wanted him to bark.

"Woof! Woof woof woof!" went Preston, sparking even more laughter from the crowd of young women.

"I think that's dog for 'I'm horny'," quipped Miss Ying, pointing at Preston's erection. More laughter ensued. "Too bad this puppy won't have a chance to sleep with me, or Miss Grace here, or any one of you. And why? Because he doesn't really *want* that. Oh, he might act like he does–he might eye-fuck you at the bar, or flirt with you, or even go along all the way to an inevitably disappointing fuck, but that's not what he wants. He *wants* to be treated like this. And that's the first lesson we have for you this evening: Some men really are dogs."

Miss Ying passed the proverbial microphone over to Miss Grace. She addressed the crowd with a beaming smile.

"Think about what a dog is. They're lovable. They're loyal. A good dog is obedient and a very good dog will shower you with affection while asking for little more in return than a warm bed, a nice meal, and maybe some old socks or something. Every man out there–the ones who put you down and make you feel small–is told they have to be these big, strong, rapey brutes. But we have evidence right in front of us that men who would be considered very, very powerful in the corporate world are most at home taking orders. And he's not the only one, ladies. I've seen *hundreds* of men come through here, looking to be dominated. And while some might not actually want to be ordered to act like a dog, they all want to be dominated in some way–usually a way they will never, ever admit out loud. Not at first, anyway."

Miss Ying clasped her hands together, picking up where Miss Grace left off.

"The reason this is our first lesson is because you can't trust what you see out there. Men aren't being honest with you. But take control, show them who's boss, and keep them heeled to what *you* want, and you'll quickly discover there are a LOT of men happy to be beneath you." Miss Ying rested a hand possessively on Preston's head, drumming her fingers on his scalp. "Just like this one here."

A hand shot up from the crowd, belonging to a woman with a powdered face and exotic eye makeup. Miss Ying pointed to her and she stood up to ask her question.

"Isn't this just catering to the male gaze all over again? Giving them what *they* want?" she asked. Several other women nodded throughout the room.

Miss Ying and Miss Grace glanced at each other, deciding how to respond.

"Well, it may start that way but it doesn't end like that," said Miss Ying. "Out there is different than in here, but in here, you inch a man more and more along what he thinks his limit is. As you do so, you mold and shape him, making him into what you want. You give him less of what he wants or make him only receive it in exchange for doing something he explicitly *doesn't* want. An hour ago we had a sharp metal hook in this puppy's nose that we used to get him to crawl around a room for us. I can assure you, he didn't like it. And what did he get in exchange for all that? He got a whiff between Miss Grace's legs."

A murmur spread throughout the crowd, but Miss Ying pushed through it.

"If your young adult experience is anything like mine was," said Miss Ying. "You know that a sniff isn't never enough for most men out there. First they want a sniff, then they want to fuck you so that *they* can feel good. But here, with someone like our puppy here, a sniff is a reward. The transaction is calculated in our favor, always."

"And as for out there," said Miss Grace, jumping in. "You need to consider your context. It might be shaping a boyfriend to be more attentive to your needs or bending a boss's will until they're empowering you. It's hard to give a one size fits all answer here, but the idea is universal–lead with what you want, use what they want to start the bait and switch, and then keep patiently shaping them until you win."

Preston vaguely realized they were blatantly describing what they were doing to him, but rather than feeling like he was seeing how a magic trick was performed, he felt… fine. Almost proud of having been the subject of their ministrations. And it was *that* thought that terrified him–if he was fine now, just getting a sniff, what would he be like after this visit to the Silk Dungeon was over?

"Any other burning questions?" asked Miss Ying. "We'll save time for Q&A later, but we understand if there's something pressing on your mind." No other hands went up. Miss Ying continued. "Onto the second lesson, and this one comes straight from Behavioral Psychology: Positive punishment. Do we have any psych majors in the room who might like to explain what positive punishment is?"

A few hands went up and Miss Ying picked a pretty girl dressed in prim, expensive-looking clothing. She stood up and addressed the room.

"Positive punishment is used to discourage undesirable or 'incorrect' responses in an experiment," she explained in Korean-accented English. "For example, if there is a box and one side can get hot and the other can't, a researcher will make the side that can get hot very hot when the subject goes near it to teach the subject what not to do."

"That's absolutely right," said Miss Ying. "I love Behavioral Psychology and think it's an especially effective tool for dealing with men."

Miss Ying turned to Preston, the joy she exhibited towards the crowd curdling into severity. She toed her boot between his legs, digging the tip in roughly. Of course Preston flinched and closed his legs and when he did, Miss Ying pulled her boot back and then slapped him hard across the face, the blow stunning him. She went to toe him again, digging in even harder this time, and when Preston flinched again, she slapped him again. Finally, the third time he kept his legs spread, even as the toe of Miss Ying's boot felt like a dull knife stabbing against his taint. He wiggled in discomfort until she was satisfied and then left her foot there, Preston's balls resting on her boots.

"See? He's learned that if he resists me, he's punished. Granted, he will still feel discomfort–after all, it's my right to exercise my will I see fit–but he now knows the way to minimize his discomfort is to allow me access to his body," Miss Ying explained. "Repeating behavior like this for men–

from pushing them away if they're too handsy and denying them sex that night to making wear a large butt plug to bed every time he forgets to flush the toilet–creates connections in his brain that associate what you want him to do with how things will feel if he doesn't do them. Isn't that right, puppy?"

Preston barked a "Woof!" and the crowd chuckled.

"See, he didn't bark a few hours ago," said Miss Ying. "But we've taught him he's our dog and somewhere in that tiny dog brain he understands what will happen if he doesn't behave as we see fit."

"And to reinforce lesson one," added Miss Grace. "This puppy–this man–paid almost $30,000 just to be here until tomorrow." The crowd broke out into shocked chatter at that. "He was even given a chance to be treated milder–kinder–but insisted we treat him like this."

Miss Ying bounced the top of her boot against Preston's balls, savoring her mastery over him.

"Remember, number one: They want and deserve this," said Miss Ying, recapping. "Number two: Use punishment to guide them towards what *you* want. And finally, number three: offer rewards strategically, but make sure those rewards have less objective value than they do subjective value." She held a hand out to Miss Grace, deferring to her Korean partner to continue.

"I said I gave this puppy a sniff as a reward for his behavior. Now I'm going to offer him something else…"

Preston watched in a daze as Miss Grace kicked off her tall officer's boots, letting them fall over on the stage. She stood and the crowd joined Preston in his confused haze as she undid her pants and pulled them off her juicy, pale legs, the pink ruffle satin thong she had on just a shimmery patch between her legs.. As she did so, Miss Ying slipped off stage to get something, coming back a minute later with a plate of piping hot food for Miss Grace and a dog bowl for Preston, An empty dog bowl.

"Excuse me for a few minutes," said Miss Grace, accepting the plate of food with a thank you. "I had an early lunch and I'm *famished*." She ate the food–some kind of Thai or Chinese chicken fried rice, it looked like–letting the crowd wonder where she was going with all this. Preston stole glances at her bare legs, getting more and more excited. Was she going to let him touch her? Maybe lick her? He imagined having his face burned between her creamy legs, the crowd watching as he ate her out.

His cock got very, very hard.

"One thing I've learned working with puppies," said Miss Grace between bites. "Is that they get hungry so often. You have to make sure you feed them several times a day, or else they can get bratty." She leaned over and scooped some of her fried rice into the dog bowl. Preston's mouth was still zipped up tight, an easy sign that he was not supposed to eat the food yet–no matter how much his stomach was starting to grumble. Miss Grace continued eating her fried rice, letting Miss Ying take over.

"But it's also very important you don't feed puppies table scraps," said Miss Ying. "For those of you who have dogs, maybe you've seen those bitter apple sprays that you use to spray down food that falls off the table. But Miss Grace and I have another method we like to use…"

Miss Ying picked up the bowl and held it towards Miss Grace. To Preston's horror he watched as Miss Grace chewed her food and spit it out into the bowl. She took another mouthful, chewed it up, and spit that into the bowl too. Miss Ying borrowed Miss Grace's fork to mix up all the food. Then, just when Preston thought it couldn't get any worse, Miss Ying gathered up a mouthful of spit and dropped it into the bowl. Miss Grace did the same.

"We'd better let this cool," said Miss Ying, setting the bowl on the stage and letting Preston get a good look at what was inside while Miss Grace finished the last of her food. They took questions from the crowd, frittering away twenty minutes fielding hypotheticals and addressing overly anecdotal concerns from the gathered women. Preston barely paid attention to it, that's how transfixed he was on the cold, half-chewed, spit-streaked food in the dog bowl.

They're going to have me eat that, he thought with a chill. *In front of all these young, pretty Asian girls.*

He caught Miss Grace looking at him with a gleaming grin. "Hungry, puppy?" she asked him.

Preston gave her as despondent of a look as he could manage through the leather hood. She laughed to herself.

"Oh I'm sure we can find something else for you if you *really* don't want it," she said, making a show of stretching out her bare legs. The insinuation was clear–no obedience, no reward. "Is that what you want?"

Thinking of his face buried deep in Miss Grace's pussy, Preston gave a grunting, low bark, the most negative sounding dog-like noise he could manage.

"So you'll eat your very special meal?" she asked him.

Preston barked enthusiastically, heart pounding at having to eat someone else's chewed-up, discarded food. Miss Grace unzipped the full length of the mouth of his leather hood, pulling the leather down and snapping it to the hood to free Preston's mouth and chin. She pushed the dog bowl towards him with her bare foot. The crowd was watching intently, gossiping amongst themselves as Preston bent down towards the "meal" Miss Grace had prepared for him.

Then he started to eat.

The taste of the food wasn't nearly as horrific as the thought of what he was doing. He tasted the rice–a nice, lightly spicy green curry fried rice with chicken–along with the vaguely sweet taste of what Preston thought was lip gloss or candy mints or perfume, some soft, female flavor that made choking down the food easier than he would've thought. The crowd, however, was losing their minds. There were gasps and disgusted cries from the women, the chatter quickly rising to a cacophonous din that Preston was grateful to not be able to decipher. Eventually there was little enough food left in the bowl that he was having trouble getting it up. Miss Grace held the bowl in place with her feet while Miss Ying pushed his head down with the bottom of her boot, "helping" him lap up every last scrap until the bowl was spic and span.

And then he was done with his degradation, his stomach sated and his ego pulverized by what he had just subjected himself to.

He looked to Miss Grace for his reward.

"Gooooood job, puppy," she cooed, her praise warm and effusive. "You finished all of it!"

There was a collective groan from the crowd, mixed with shocked, horrified laughter. Preston felt tiny before them, and even though he was richer than many–if not all–of them would ever be, he felt pathetic compared to them, like he truly was part of some lower caste that groveled and begged for their discards.

"I guess you deserve a treat," said Miss Grace as she brought the conversation back to lesson number three.

Preston's cock pulsed with excitement. *Finally*, he thought.

She picked up the dog bowl, collecting another mouthful of spit to drop into it. Miss Ying did the same.

What's going on? wondered Preston.

Miss Grace set the bowl back down and stepped her foot into it, getting their joint spit all over the sole of her foot and between her toes. She slung her leg over the arm of the chair and held her foot out to Preston.

"There you go, puppy. Your dessert."

He looked at her with a kernel of anger in his eyes. She'd intentionally misled him, making him think his "reward" would be something much more intimate instead of just her spit-covered foot. She wiggled her toes at him.

"Are you full?" she asked mockingly. The Korean gave him a full-lipped, glossy smirk. "You can skip dessert if you are."

Still stewing that he had humiliated himself so much for *this*, Preston remained quiet and motionless. Neither mistress said anything. Then Miss Grace started to pull her foot away, calling his bluff.

Preston craned his neck forward, lolling out his tongue. He ran it down the length of Miss Grace's sole, from her heel all the way to the ball of her foot, tasting the sweat and spit and foot odor along the delicate, creased skin. Miss Grace giggled.

"Puppies love licking feet," she said to the crowd. "The smellier and sweatier, the better."

Preston's tongue found the spaces between Miss Grace's toes, and as he cleaned away the lint and spit there, he felt his excitement mounting. He drew one of her toes into his mouth and sucked, hard, twirling his tongue around the toe, feeling the mix of rough skin texture and smooth painted nails under his tongue.

Miss Grace shifted her other leg to hang over the edge of the armchair, and used her free foot to tease Preston's cock. He panted, pushing himself against her foot as best he could, feeling like a horny, brainless animal. He took a few of her toes into his mouth, including her big toe, and frantically ran his tongue along them and then sucked them all at once as Miss Grace snatched his shift between her toes, lightly stroking him.

"See now *this* is the kind of reward a good puppy deserves," Miss Grace told the crowd.

And even though it wasn't what Preston had wanted, her words rang true for him. He voraciously sucked her toes, one by one, while Miss Grace brought him closer and closer to the edge with her free foot. The silicone plug tail whapped against Preston's ass as he did his best to hump into her spread-toe pumping, managing to pull his hips back enough to get Miss Grace to tease his swollen, precum-dripping head. He huffed and puffed as he wildly licked Miss Grace's foot, planting kisses along the sides of her sole and then down to the heel, where he sucked on the sweaty, warm skin.

"Remember, rewards should be subjectively valuable to the man, and not objectively valuable to you. Letting a man fuck you, and giving away your pussy… that's a *big*, valuable reward. Too valuable if you ask me. But letting him lick your foot—or buy you a pair of panties you were on a date or see you in a revealing dress during a meeting—that's something that isn't expensive for you, not really. But if you train him, it *can* be very valuable to him."

Preston felt himself getting close; just another minute and he'd pop all over Miss Grace's foot. He sped up his humping, his panting so loud now the girls in the crowd could hear it clearly.

Miss Ying cleared her throat, rising above Preston's desperate panting. "Also remember that the rewards must be strategically given…and never overindulged in."

Miss Grace pulled her feet away, the one Preston was licking and the one between his legs. He was stunned and looked at her blankly for a few moments. A spark of anger floated up through him and as if reading his mind, Miss Grace shot him a daring glance. Preston backed down and accepted that the mistress had pulled her feet away.

"I think I'm good now," she said, like she'd pushed aside a bowl of popcorn instead of leaving Preston blueballed on the verge of cumming. Miss Grace shifted over and rezipped Preston's leather hood, covering his mouth again and giving him a victorious smile. He watched helplessly as she pulled her pants back over her creamy legs, cleaning her feet off with a hand towel before she put her socks and boots on.

Miss Ying clapped her hands together. "Moving on. If you'd like to participate in the play session, please form a line at the right side of the stage. Miss Grace, when you're ready, can you gather what we'll need? I'll get our puppy ready."

Preston was still yearning to cum when Miss Ying leaned in closer and whispered: "Time to have some fun with you, puppy."

THE NEW TOY

A dozen or so women had lined up by the stage, the others going heavy on wine as they watched the stage. Preston was watching in nervous anticipation too, wondering what the mistresses might have in store for him. Miss Ying pushed the armchairs and the doggy bed towards the back of the stage, creating plenty of space just as Miss Grace returned with what looked like a large canvas roll-up kit, the sort used to transport chef's tools. Only this one was two feet long and much bulkier than the ones Preston had seen before.

Miss Grace set it on the side of the stage where the young Asian girls were queued up, unfurling it to reveal an assortment of canes, paddles, crops, and other tools of discipline. Preston's heart sank, knowing there could only be one intended target in this room for those.

"A few fun facts about our puppy guest of honor," Miss Ying told the room. "He's in his mid-40s, works for one of the richest companies in the world, and, including stock options, made nearly $1.5M last year."

As Preston started to wonder how she could possibly know that, he remembered that he had disclosed his salary information to Mistress Midori while he was filling out paperwork for the Omakase Package. The women queued up didn't look pleased with these facts, and two more stood up from the tables to get in line.

"Despite this privilege he has," continued Miss Ying. "We are going to give each of you a moment of catharsis with him, inviting you to take thirty seconds to do whatever you would like to him."

Preston's blood turned to ice. Was she serious?

Miss Grace added: "We encourage you to be creative and inventive with how you spend your time. There are no second chances, so use your thirsty seconds wisely!"

One of the girls waiting in line, the primly dressed girl with the Korean-accented English, raised her hand. Miss Grace nodded to her and she asked, "Is it really whatever we like?"

"Well… obviously we don't want you to *really* hurt him," said Miss Ying. "So we ask you just use the tools up here and your own bodies. But there's a lot you can do with your own body."

By way of demonstration, Miss Ying reached down and snatched Preston's nipple in her gloved fingers. As she squeezed hard, he grunted in pain, caught between the urge to pull away and not further invoke Miss Ying's cruelty. When she let go, he saw the queued women nodding, inspired by the Chinese mistress's quick-thinking.

"If anyone needs more time, feel free to let others go ahead of you," encouraged Miss Grace.

The women mulled about in thought, allowing one towards the back to walk her way to the front of the queue. She was an athletic-looking girl with a sorority girl's smile, her dyed-blonde hair pulled back in a ponytail. She marched up the stairs with confidence and ignored the opened roll-up kit, getting close to Preston and pushing him back onto his heels. The girl reached between his legs and pinched the head of his cock, squeezing her fingers together as hard as she could. Preston instinctively tried to pull away, but she held on firm, slapping his balls with her other hand as she watched him flail in pain. Her slaps grew harder, until Preston was grunting and almost shouting at her to stop under his leather hood.

When a soft chime went off, signaling the end of the athletic girl's thirty seconds, Preston breathed a sigh of relief. She gave him one last slap–the hardest yet–and then marched off stage and back to her seat to pour herself a fresh glass of wine.

She hadn't said a word the entire time.

Miss Ying chuckled and addressed the audience: "See how easy that was? Who's next?"

A girl made her way to the front of the line, a tanned, Hawaiian type with a warm smile and an easygoing way about her. She looked through the roll-up kit items and took out a slender, beige fiberglass wand that looked like a conductor's baton. She approached Preston and flicked the baton at him.

"Sit," she said, her voice as honeyed and soothing as her looks.

Preston sat back on his heels, nervously keeping his legs spread open. His balls still hurt.

"Good boy!" the girl cooed. She held out her hand and flicked the baton at Preston's hand.

"Paw," she said.

Preston extended out his mittened hand, setting it in the tanned girl's palm. She gave him a bright smile.

"Very good!" she said. "Let's see, what else can I have you do…"

"Fifteen seconds," said Miss Ying.

Getting an idea, the girl pointed the baton at her leg and said: "Hump."

The girls in the crowd giggled at the command, but Preston, slipping deeper and deeper into this animal mindset, took it with deadly seriousness; it didn't hurt that the Hawaiian-looking girl had lean, long legs that were covered in shiny nylon stockings.

Preston inched forward and pushed himself up against her, the nylon delightful on his abused and denied shaft. He rutted away, the tanned girl, laughing at the sight of him. Miss Ying called time and she pulled her leg away, leaving Preston hard and wanting.

The next fifteen minutes were a nonstop parade of women coming on stage to degrade Preston. He was spanked and clawed at by a Chinese girl with long red nails; forced to roll over and beg by the primly dressed Korean girl, who rewarded his efforts with a surprising scattershot blast of spit in his face; caned on his feet by a Thai woman who yelled incomprehensible insults at him; slapped until his ears rang and his vision was glassy by the curvy half-Asian with the gently parted lips; made to sniff at a Japanese girl's denim-clad ass, Preston quickly discovering she had farted just before she got on stage; kicked in the balls so hard he shouted for mercy by a petite woman in all black, with pink hair and plenty of piercings.

By the time the line was down to its last person, Preston's head was racing, his ass and cock and balls aching, his body covered in sweat and bright red marks given to him by the army of 20-something girls.

The final woman came off as somehow different from the others, and seemed to have waited to go last. She was frighteningly confident in her sleek, high-fashion business wear–tailored black blazer, cream-colored blouse, pencil skirt with dark nylons, expensive-looking heels–and just a hair shorter than Miss Ying, with a powerful, vivacious frame. Large was the wrong word for it, though she was certainly *not* petite. Her straight black hair was cut into a short lob and she had smooth features, made smoother by her matte makeup, cherry red lips, and carefully-lined eyes done up to exaggerate their almond shape. A dusting of faint freckles were scattered across the bridge of her nose and cheeks.

The woman took her time looking over the roll-up kit of tortuous tools and then pulled out a long, black riding crop, sauntering up to Preston.

"All fours," she snapped at him.

He assumed a position on his mittened hands and padded knees. The woman stepped to the side of him and he braced himself for the sting of the crop.

It landed where Preston had least expected–right on the silicone butt plug. He felt its bulbous head push against his prostate and there was a warm surge up his shaft that felt surprisingly good. She cropped him against the plug, exactly in the same spot, and there was another surge. After being teased and denied on stage by Miss Grace and a handful of the women from the crowd, each push of the plug against him was bliss. Either the woman intuited this or already knew it, because the cropping picked up speed, pushing the plug against that sensitive spot inside him faster and faster.

Preston didn't know how much time there was left in the woman's thirty seconds when he came. But he did cum, all over the stage, to the shrieks and hollers of the watching women. As soon as he started to squirt, the woman pulled the crop away, leaving Preston helpless as his cock pumped out a puddle of seed below him. His ass spasmed around the plug, driving it against him even without the help of the crop, and Preston moaned into the hood. Looking pleased with herself, the woman strode to the side of the stage, put the crop back, and went to sit down.

"Naughty puppy," said Miss Grace, once she had gotten hold of her own surprise.

"*Very* naughty," said Miss Ying. The tall, Chinese mistress was less surprised than she was irritated. "Didn't we talk about this? Did you have permission to release?"

Preston hung his head low, remembering how Miss Ying had forced him to hold in the enema and how insistent she was about her control of his body. Miss Ying crouched down next to Preston and forced his head back up.

"Do you remember what I said I'd do if you had an accident?" she asked him as she unzipped the lower part of Preston's leather hood. She snapped it open against the collar. "Well? Do you?"

Preston whimpered quietly. He remembered full well.

"Don't complain to me," said Miss Ying. "*You're* the one who made a mess. And now you're going to clean it up."

With her gloved hand, Miss Ying scooped up a palmful of Preston's spilt seed and held it up to his mouth. She gave him a hard stare.

"Don't make me wait. I'm being nice about this—for now," she said.

His face contorted into a grimace, Preston reached his tongue down and licked the mess out of Miss Ying's hand. It was bitter and salty and he gagged as he brought it into his mouth to swallow. The crowd was whipped into a frenzy now, half the girls unable to watch while the other half looked on with morbid curiosity. He heard bits and pieces of their chatter through the rising costs:

"Is he really doing this?"

"Omigod this is so gross!"

"He PAID for this??"

"Ugh, I *hate* when my boyfriend cums in my mouth…"

"I can't believe she's making him lick it up!"

Preston licked Miss Ying's gloved hand clean, only for her to scoop up another palmful, then another and another. When there wasn't enough left for her to scoop up, she forced his face down, making him lick it right off the stage. By the time he was done, his tongue was filthy from the dirt and grit on the floor and his mouth tasted of a mix of cum and chalky dust. Miss Grace came forward and clipped the leash back on. She started to lead him off stage.

"Let's have a round of applause for our very special guest of honor!" said Miss Ying.

The room burst into sarcastic applause as Miss Grace led him down the stage and past the horseshoe of tables, the women whistling and hooting and yelling snide insults at him all the way to the elevator. The doors closed to the sound of their ferocious, mocking clapping, the young girls rising to a standing ovation. Then Preston was alone with the Korean mistress in the elevator. He felt small and pitiful.

"You know, when we were planning that little event upstairs, Miss Ying *really* wanted us to get someone from your company to be there, someone you would recognize," Miss Grace said, flipping back her wavy, honey brown hair. "Midori was on board and the other mistresses didn't really care either way. I talked them out of it."

"Thank you," Preston croaked, forgetting for a minute their demeaning dog roleplay.

"You're very welcome, puppy. Maybe you'll have a chance to properly thank me later."

The doors opened a few floors below and they exited onto a subdued hallway with red carpeting and dim mood lighting. The doors here looked less like the ones downstairs, where Mistress Midori's office and the other playrooms were. They looked almost like apartment or hotel room doors, each numbered in cursive, woodblock lettering. Miss Grace brought Preston to room 1119 at the end of the hallway. She took a key off her belt ring and opened it.

Inside it really did look like a hotel room, complete with upholstered furniture in a main room with an adjoining bathroom. There was a big bed against the wall, facing a TV, with a table to its side set for dinner for two. One chair was fitted with heavy leather cuffs.

As Preston tried to guess what this was all for, Miss Grace began taking off his puppy garments. His legs cried out in sore pain as she undid the thigh-bindings and it felt so good to finally be able to move his fingers freely again. The hood came off next, Preston's hair drenched in sweat. Then Miss Grace brought him to the bathroom, to take out the plug and wipe down whatever lube clung to his ass and the backs of his legs. Her motions were gentle and caring, and something about the way she handled him made Preston all the more nervous for why he was here in this hotel-like room.

She sat him at the dining table, cuffing his wrists and ankles to the chair. Before she left, she turned on the TV and raised the volume.

"Enjoy, puppy," she said to him as she stepped back out into the hallway.

On TV, Preston saw some elaborate fetish movie start to play. It was in Japanese and it opened on some kind of manor in the countryside that seemed to belong to a Japanese woman in her late 30s or maybe early 40s, dressed in a black cocktail dress with a string of pearls around her neck. She had a coterie of female staff and friends–a butler, some kind of equestrian trainer type, a duo in their own cocktail dresses–as well as a whole host of men in nothing but tight black underwear with hoods on their heads, who were scampering at her feet, attending to her every need.

Preston watched, transfixed as the woman found excuse after excuse to torment and belittle the men with extreme, unthinkable measures. He wished he could turn away or even just change the channel or lower the volume, but he was forced to watch and listen as he waited for whoever would be joining him on the other side of the table. He prayed that the bizarre fetish happenings on screen weren't a sign of what was to come.

ROOM 1119

After fifteen or twenty minutes–much like in the rest of the Silk Dungeon, there were no clocks in this room–the door opened. In walked Mistress Midori, still in her sleeveless emerald dress that hugged her curvy, voluptuous body. Her stockings swished as she took the seat across from Preston. She gave him a polite smile.

"Hi there," she said. "It's so lovely to have you join me for dinner tonight. Do you like steak?"

Mistress Midori pressed a small white button on the table that Preston hadn't noticed until now.

"Not in a chatty mood?" she asked, the fetish video loud with the wailing of a man who was taking a whipping from the lady of the manor, long red streaks left behind with each crack of the expertly-wielded whip.

Mistress Midori noticed Preston looking at the screen.

"Oh, let me lower that." She stood up and grabbed the remote, taking the volume down. She smoothed her dress before she sat back down.

There was a knock on the door. A few seconds later it opened and a female Asian waiter came in holding a tray. She said something in Japanese and then set the tray down on the table, removing its domed steel cloche to reveal a gorgeous cut of meat. Preston could smell the rich scent of the steak, along with the pad of butter atop it. Next to the meat were herbed potatoes, broccoli, and a clove of fried garlic. Preston's mouth watered, but with his hands cuffed to the chair, there was no way for him to reach for the utensils in front of him. The female waiter filled their glasses with ruby-colored wine before bowing and leaving the two to their meal.

Mistress Midori cut herself a piece of steak and took a bite, savoring it with closed eyes and a happy sigh.

"*Oisihii*," she said. "Delicious."

Preston watched as the mistress helped herself to a little more steak along with some of the vegetables while in the background, the fetish video transitioned to a scene in the shower. The lady of the manor was naked now, along with one of her friends, and they were being bathed by a scampering male. It wasn't long before they had his face in their wild, ungroomed bushes, servicing them as they laughed and chatted.

"I hope you've been enjoying your Omakase so far," said Mistress Midori. "We put a lot of work into it to get it just right." She made a show of looking over at Preston's empty plate. "Maybe you'd prefer if I chewed the steak up first for you?" she asked with a snide laugh.

Of course she knew about that. The thought that Mistress Midori knew about the last few hours made him feel shy and sheepish. He looked at the steak longingly and then back at the mistress, wondering if she was just going to make him watch her eat all night.

She spoke to him with her mouth half-full. "You know, the results from your personality assessment were very interesting. As I understand it, usually for your sort there's some underlying theme in the data where the subject projects not wanting to have control but secretly desires to control things from a leveraged position. 'Topping from the bottom' is the term we use, and one you might be familiar with. But with you, you actually yearn for a loss of control, although your tests suggest you have strong walls up to keep you from having to accept such a loss. As much as you might say you want to give up control, if left to your devices you will hold onto it. And that means we have to break those walls down."

Mistress Midori set her fork and knife down and took a sip of the wine. She studied him with her dark eyes.

"Preston, would you like some steak?"

"Yes," he murmured. "Please."

She cut off a small piece and held it out to him across the table. He took it in his mouth and chewed. It was fantastic, perfectly seared and simply melt-in-his-mouth perfect. Much as the mistress had done, he savored it with a satisfied, relaxed sigh.

"See? That wasn't so hard, was it?" She took another sip of her wine. "Would you like another piece?"

"Yes please," Preston was quick to say.

"Maybe later," said Mistress Midori.

And just like that, she had set the rules: Mistress Midori was the giver– and denier–of wonderful things. Preston could ask, but asking was no guarantee he would receive. The mistress dug her tongue around her mouth, working out a piece of meat from between her teeth.

"How did you put it earlier? You wanted an experience that would reveal something about yourself you couldn't get in a meeting room? Surely the session upstairs wasn't *that* far away from being in a meeting, was it? And I bet you learned a few things about yourself. If nothing else, you know what your semen tastes like now."

Mistress Midori cut another piece of steak for herself. The fetish video had switched to a scene outside, where the men were being forced to pull a cart with the lady of the manor in it, who had since changed into an equestrian blazer, jodhpurs, and a tweed hunting cap. They had elaborate headdresses with feathers and bits that make them look like ponies, with long horsehair plugs driven deep in their asses. The lady of the many had a thin riding whip and used it with abandon to make the men go faster and faster.

"I can tell Miss Grace really likes you," said the mistress. "She's cute, isn't she?"

She watched as Preston ignored the question, clearly already thinking it.

"Yes, she's very cute," continued Mistress Midori. "So many of our clients seem to wind up with a crush on her it seems. She's got that teasing, warm, maybe-she-will energy to her, doesn't she? It's hardly a surprise her boyfriend is unbelievably hot, one of those big, muscled guys with a Prince Charming face."

Preston's shoulders slumped. Of course someone like her would be with some jockish pretty boy. That had been the other story of Preston's life–always winding up on the nerdy side of the fence, envying the naturally tall, athletic guys who seemed to be able to get any girl they wanted. When he'd been in school, the girls those guys went after were the perfect, pretty cheerleader sort. That was part of how Preston had started getting into Asian girls in the first place–they were the ones with interests more like his, the ones who were smart and who didn't often fit into the jock-y American culture of his youth. But thinking about Asian girls like Miss Grace–confident, sultry, drop dead gorgeous–being taken by the jocks of the world made him stew bitterly.

"Oh, don't look so disappointed," said Mistress Midori. "You're not her type anyway. She likes them to be true alphas–young, dumb, and full of cum. Though I guess that last night might apply to you after what happened upstairs." The Japanese mistress chuckled. "Funny thing, actually. Most professional mistresses aren't into the submissive guys. Though you know who does? Miss Ying. I heard she once made an ex of hers wear a diaper and stayed handcuffed to the radiator for pissing her off while she went out drinking and dancing. She came back and the poor bastard was starving, with a soiled diaper, sitting in the dark waiting for her. *That's* how she likes her relationships."

The Japanese mistress put her utensils down and pushed out her chair, unlocking the table's wheels to move it away from Preston. She picked up the TV remote and changed the station, moving away from the fetish video to another film. This one featured a man with his arms secured up over his head, left to stand on his tippy toes. An Asian woman with bikini tan lines and tied-up, long, straight black hair walked around him, teasing and poking him as he tried to keep his balance.

"I love the way men's brains are wired," she said, as she watched the porn with him. "They can be so brilliant when their lust is calm, so calculated and patient and clever. But once their libidos kick in, it's like a completely different persona."

Mistress Midori snaked her hand between Preston's legs and played with his cock, quickly getting him nice and hard. Her teasing became a firm, slow stroking as Preston's breathing got heavy. He watched on screen as the Asian reached around behind the man and toyed with his cock. "Do you want to fuck me, big boy?" It was hammy and theatrical, but it stoked Preston's lust nonetheless. He rocked his hips against Mistress Midori's hand, trying to urge her to pump faster. She maintained a painstakingly steady pace.

"See, Preston, I'm not going to let you cum. I'm telling you this directly, honestly, so that you know it for a fact. And since I've told you it, there should be no reason for you to keep staring at the screen or trying to push into me, or doing anything but–logically–asking me to stop. But that's not what you're going to do, is it?"

Preston watched as the woman moved in front of the man, slipping his cock between her ass cheeks, leaving it standing up so that he could not penetrate her. She bent over, dangling the promise of fucking her, and looked into the camera seductively. Preston's chest was tight now and his body warm. He moved his hips as much as his bindings in the chair would allow, some little corner of his brain hoping the mistress might make a miscalculation or have mercy on him, giving him the chance to cum again, but this time without a big plug in his ass.

Mistress Midori let go of him.

She stepped around to the edge of the bed, the movie playing behind her, and reached back to unzip the back of her shimmery emerald dress. It came off like a snakeskin. Underneath, the curvy Japanese mistress had on a matching bright white lace bra and panty set with intricate floral designs across the sheer lace. Between her legs Preston could see a pillow patch of jet black hair. She sat down on the bed, opening her legs wide, and began playing with herself through her panties. Preston's head pingponged between the screen–now a close up of the man trying to rub himself off deep in the woman's ass cheeks–and Mistress Midori luxuriating in the circular rubbing touch of her fingers.

Preston's cock pulsed with need. He watched her greedily as she let out a husky breath, eyes tracing the swelling curves of her full breasts and swelled hips and smooth thighs. He pulled against his cuffs and hated how he couldn't even stroke himself. On screen, the woman wiggled her ass back onto the man and let out a lewd moan. Mistress Midori fluttered her eyes at him deviously.

"Should I stop?" she asked him.

"No," Preston said, desperate.

"No, of course not," she said, laughing. "God, I love men."

The mistress leaned forward and opened the top drawer of the nightstand next to the bed. She pulled out a pink-and-red vibrator wand and flicked it on, the wand's large head buzzing to life. Mistress Midori brought it to her already-wet panties and smiled as the vibrating drum pressed against her. Preston's attention was fully on her now, ignoring the scenes on TV. Slowly, the smell of her sex filled the room and Preston inhaled it eagerly, his mind a jumble of wants and desires.

When she came it was loud and unabashed. Mistress Midori fell back on the bed, tossing aside the vibrator, and caught her breath.

"Do you want to know what my pussy tastes like?" she asked him.

Silence yawned between them. Was she serious? If Preston said yes, would she let him put his tongue on her? Or was this just another piece of steak that she would deny him?

"I asked you a question, *Mr.* Walton. Would you like to know what my pussy tastes like?"

"Yes," Preston said.

"Ask me then. Tell me how much you'd enjoy that," said Mistress Midori in a breathy, smiling voice.

"I… want to know what your pussy tastes like," said Preston, his heart beating fast. Of all the things he had been through already, somehow this was one of the most exposing. No hoods, no roleplay–just him speaking out loud a taboo desire. "I'd like to–love to–taste you."

"Taste you who? Who am I?" asked the mistress.

"I'd love to taste you… M-mistress Midori," said Preston.

"Mistress. That's a powerful word, isn't it? Just saying it reinforces a very specific dynamic: Mistress and submissive. Say it again."

"Mistress," said Preston. The act of saying it made him throb for her, made him slip into a strange head state of *wanting* to do anything she asked.

"Mmmm. I adore the sound of that word. I guess I can comply with your request," Mistress Midori said.

She sat up and smiled mischievously at Preston as she reached down to pull off her white, wet panties. The silky black hair between her legs was dewy and glistening, and Preston could just make out the delicate slit of her pussy lips.

"Ready?" she asked him.

Preston nodded eagerly.

Mistress Midori got up off the bed and pressed her balled up panties to Preston's mouth, shoving them inside. She patted him on the head.

"There you go. Enjoy," she said as she went to the bathroom to clean herself up.

Preston whined into the panties, the heady, musky taste of the mistress flooding his senses. It was like concentrated nectar perfume and sweet sweat mixed together, and even though Preston had wanted so much more, he still savored getting to suck on the soaked lace underwear.

Mistress Midori came back a few minutes later with a fresh pair of panties on. They were made of white satin and underneath them Preston could see the fluff of her full bush. She took her time getting dressed again, completely ignoring Preston, and then had one more sip of wine before she put her heels back on. Before she left, she flipped through the TV channels. Every single channel was playing one Asian femdom video or another and the mistress finally settled on what looked like a CCTV feed. Mistress Midori gave him a cheeky wave and left the room.

With a jolt, Preston realized it was a recording of him with Miss Ying and Miss Grace in the doggy playroom.

TIGER, BEAT

The CCTV footage was set to loop, giving Preston plenty of time to watch his degrading behavior again and again and again. The initial embarrassment he felt watching himself faded by the third or fourth loop, allowing him to spend the time ogling the women and–he couldn't believe he was thinking this–wishing he were dressed up as Miss Grace and Miss Ying's puppy again.

When the room's door lock turned, Preston looked over, expecting to see Mistress Midori–or maybe even Miss Grace, or Miss Ying. But instead it was the woman from the dinner seminar upstairs, the one in the sleek business outfit, with the powerful frame, short lob haircut, and smooth face dusted with freckles.

The one who had cropped the plug in his ass until he came all over the stage.

He went to ask her "I don't think you should be here?", forgetting he still had Mistress Midori's panties in his mouth. Instead it came out as a muffled cry of worry.

The curvaceous woman gave a deep laugh. She looked over at the TV. The loop was up to the part where Miss Ying was leading Preston around in circles by the hook-leash in his nose. She nodded approvingly.

"Pain is the greatest motivator throughout all of human history," she said. "Even more than sex. With sex, you can make a man get down on his knees and beg you to touch him. With pain, you can make a man get down on his knees and beg you to stop."

Preston was beginning to think this woman was not a true member of the doe-eyed women upstairs.

"Lady Khan," she said to him. "Apologies for the subterfuge at dinner. We thought having one of us sitting with the guests would help get the conversation going and get everyone to relax."

One of us. A Silk Dungeon mistress. That explained how sure she was and how easily she–Lady Khan–was able to make Preston cum. Which meant Miss Ying and Miss Grace had to know that would happen. Preston almost wanted to laugh, thinking how much Miss Ying must've enjoyed acting annoyed, forcing Preston to lick up his own seed as punishment even though that was the plan all along…

Lady Khan turned off the TV. She came over to Preston and tweezed the panties out of his mouth, dropping them between his legs to drape over his erect cock. She undid his cuffs, but left him sitting there. He watched her body sway sensually as she turned her back on him and put her hands on her hips.

"That personality assessment you took–I was the one who designed it," she said. "I have a doctorate in Applied Behavioral Sciences and a master's in Statistics. With just two dozen questions and some machine learning, you can reasonably predict 90% of a person's basic behavior. With the assessment *you* took, well… it's practically mind-reading at that point. I might know you better than you know yourself by this point."

Lady Khan tapped her fingers against one hip. Preston took in the sight of the statuesque, indomitable woman, thinking how she could likely wrestle him to the ground with ease, if she wanted to. His balls ached dully. Maybe a part of *him* wanted her to, he wondered.

"Naturally, I read up on you," Lady Khan continued. "You've earned yourself a nice little reputation in the tech circles. I don't care much for all that product management, growth-hacking nonsense that goes on in your line of work, but the statistician in me can appreciate the complexity involved. I was even more amused to see we both went to Princeton."

Preston couldn't help himself: "You're a Tiger?"

Her back still turned to him, Lady Khan nodded. "Class of '13. You were what, '99?"

"Yeah…" Preston did the math. If Lady Khan graduated in 2013, that made her 30, maybe 31. Her domineering stature aside, Preston would've guessed she was half a decade younger than that.

I must be getting old, he thought.

"The last of the 20th century crop," said Lady Khan. "It must twist your mind into a pretzel to see all those college girls upstairs who weren't even alive by the time you graduated, huh?"

Now that she mentioned it, it did.

"Especially when you hooded and plugged up on stage," she added. She huffed a laugh. "Though you and I both know you have mid-level teleiophilic tendencies, with a statistically significant innate desire to yield authority to sexually mature, yet youth-presenting females."

When Preston remained silent, Lady Khan looked over her shoulder at him with a smug smile.

"It means you get off on submitting to women in their early 20s," she said. Lady Khan turned, hands still on her hourglass hips. "Though that's not your only tendency, that's for sure. Your assessment also proved out a subconscious wish to roleplay having lesser intelligence–hence Miss Ying and Miss Grace's little puppy charade. What's interesting to me is that when we isolate questions from the assessment to measure for intelligence, your results are, well… pretty average."

Preston knitted his brows together. "What?" he asked.

"I know, I was surprised too," said Lady Khan. "Princeton grad, elite employment, an impressive track record of being at the hottest new companies. Given your history, *of course* I expected to see your wish to play out a 'lesser intelligence' role. But when I revisited your background in light of the isolated intelligence assessment, it made me consider that maybe you've just been in the right place at the right time, Tiger."

The way Lady Khan spoke, it felt like being at the rotten end of a bad performance review. Preston's excited erection was flagging now and he could feel a defensive heat rising up through his body.

"What exactly are you saying?" Preston asked, not afraid to challenge the woman. Who did she think she was anyway? She was a mistress–a fetish sex worker–for anyone who could afford it.

As well as someone who held a PhD and master's degree, he reminded himself.

Lady Khan let out a reluctant sigh. "I'm not trying to put you down," she said, though her tone suggested otherwise. "I'm simply saying that luck may account for more of your success than raw intelligence, maybe even most of it. Which reminds me, did you know that for the Class of '99, the Princeton acceptance rate was 13%? For this upcoming year, it's going to be a little over 4%. That means it was more than three times easier for you to get accepted into Princeton than the three girls upstairs who are freshmen there right now."

Preston did in fact not know that.

"Anyway, I'm going off on a tangent–I just love my numbers. My point is that if you ever felt like you were carrying a burden for being too smart or too distant from the rest of the world because of your intelligence, you can let it go now," said Lady Khan.

She bent forwards and looked into Preston's eyes.

"You aren't all that special," she said to him. "Which, ironically, makes you perfect for the Silk Dungeon. We, ahem, specialize in not-so-special men here." She stroked his cheek. "You fit right in with the rest of our beta boys and boot humpers and horny, little sluts."

Her stroking hand moved down Preston's chest and then his belly, wrapping itself around Mistress Midori's panties that were still draped over his now soft shaft. Lady Khan teased him with the damp lace until he stirred again. She leaned to whisper in his ear, her heavy breasts pushing against him.

"I've asked for you to stay in my room tonight," she said. "You can pretend you're back at the Princeton dorms–as long as you keep your hands to yourself."

Lady Khan continued to pump him with firm, strong, ropey strokes.

"Do you want to come and see my room now?" she asked him in a breathy whisper.

Preston nodded, the lump in his throat making it impossible for him to speak. Lady Khan righted herself, taking the damp panties off his cock and draping them instead over his head, so that the wet crotch was over his nose and mouth and he was forced to look out through the leg holes. She then turned and patted the curve of her ass in a "come follow" motion. Preston stood as if he was hypnotized and followed the mistress out of the room, his cock leading the way like a pointing compass.

Lady Khan strode down the hall, turning halfway to a branch of rooms down a short alcove. When she reached 1125, she pushed open the door, Preston following after. The layout of the room was not dissimilar to where he'd had "dinner" with Mistress Midori. Lady Khan indicated the bathroom.

"Wash up and when you're ready we'll get you ready for bed," she said.

Preston wasn't starving, but he'd been hoping for a little more food–steak or not. He glanced at the bed. It looked lush and comfortable, and he tried not to get lost in thoughts of sleeping next to the voluptuous, strapping Lady Khan. He went to wash up.

There were fresh towels, a toothbrush, and mouthwash laid out for him– along with a small card with a printed message on it in cursive script: "Touch yourself as much as you need to get clean. Nothing more. I'm watching."

Preston spun around, seeking out where a hidden camera might be tucked into a corner or next to one of the fixtures. He didn't see anything. This might be another of the Silk Dungeon's head games or Lady Khan might really be spying on him. Either way, it wasn't worth the risk. He ran the shower until the water was hot and steamy and then climbed in, relieved to feel the soothing heat on his aching, tired body.

He took a moment to reflect.

The Omakase Package. His adventure, his attempt to make up for lost time. His attempt to be someone else. It had all seemed so clear to him when he had booked the visit, but now he felt unsure. What had he expected? In his mind's eye, he had seen a theatrical, gothic dungeon with incense hanging in the air and women in corsets and catsuits putting him in a big cage, calling him names like "slave". But so far the reality of his visit had been terrifyingly personal.

He thought about his head between Miss Grace's legs, being made to suffer an enema in front of Miss Ying, sitting up like a trained dog in front of a room of attractive, young strangers. He thought of Lady Khan's words.

You aren't all that special.

His secret fear, spoken aloud.

He'd never felt like he'd earned his accolades, that was true. Princeton had been a long shot, he was a good software engineer but he'd met better, and Lady Khan was absolutely right–he had a knack for being in the right place at the right time. The first time had been a fluke–his Princeton buddy had gotten him the job at his first to-be-acquired company, but by the third time it happened, Preston had begun to drink his own Kool-Aid, thinking that *had* to be something more than just dumb luck in winding up at all these burgeoning hotspots. But he'd never figured out what that something was.

Now he was senior enough where he didn't have to fight to survive. People listened to him not because of what he did but because of who he was. Presto Lang, winner of the triple acquisition hat trick, the man with the startup Midas touch. It didn't matter that his track record of strategic decision making was spotty and that he hadn't had a big win in years. He didn't pay for it, the junior engineers and project leads did. Preston Lang just got second chance, after second chance.

He finished up his shower and toweled off, drying his hair. He felt tired. He'd been using the same line for more than a decade–"Those who compromise never achieve anything great"–but Preston knew the truth. It was just a smokescreen to hide the fact that he never really felt like he knew what he was doing.

Preston stepped back into the main room, feeling too sorry for himself to still be excited to be sleeping next to Lady Khan. Then he saw what she'd laid out on the bed: it was a long, large, black leather body bag. Lady Khan was standing next to it, her arms folded over her chest. She looked peeved.

"I thought you were going to use up all the hot water in the Dungeon," she said. "You better have not been playing with yourself."

So she wasn't watching, thought Preston.

Lady Khan shrugged. "Well, there won't be any touching tonight. Get in the bag."

"What is it…?" wondered Preston.

"What does it look like? It's a sleepsack. *Your* sleepsack. I promise you, it's very cozy."

Before his shower, Preston might've made a face or tried to appeal to Lady Khan with a pitiful look. But he felt defeated now and didn't even fight Lady Khan's command to crawl inside the sleepsack. If she noticed anything different about him, she didn't say it, zipping up the twin zippers of the sack once he was inside. The leather tightened around Preston, covering him from toe to neck. Then Lady Khan took the sleepsack's laces and pulled those tight as well, fitting the leather around Preston like a corset so that his arms were pushed against him, his legs pressed together, and his body feeling like he could only inhale and exhale.

The mistress ran her hands along the leather, feeling Preston through it before she got undressed in the dim shadows of the room's low light, taking off everything, even her tiny black thong and her scallop-edged bra. She laid down next to Preston and wrapped one leg around him, using him like a body pillow. He could feel the warmth of her crotch, even though the leather, and could smell her floral, earthy perfume wreathing the air.

"Good night," she whispered in his ear, kissing his cheek before she turned off the lights.

His sleep was restless and broken, made worse by Lady Khan's stirring touches and the feel of her body resting comfortably on his, and–despite his self-pitying–being so close to the mistress made Preston horny all over again. Only this time, with the sleepsack sausage-tight around him, his would-be erection was smothered into an uncomfortable half-mast, his poking cock yearning for freedom. No matter how he tried, he couldn't shift his hips or adjust his position the least little bit. All he could do was move his head from side to side, looking from darkness to Lady Khan's smooth, sleeping face.

Somehow, he managed to fade into a dreamless slumber. When he woke it was morning again, as the previously shuttered slit windows revealed. He was still in the sleepsack on Lady Khan's bed and he could hear her brushing her teeth in the bathroom.

"Oh you're up," she said when she came out. She was wearing a white terrycloth robe and Preston could see there was nothing on underneath. "Good, I need a little attention."

Lady Khan let the robe fall open. Preston could see now that the mistress's downy pubic hair was groomed into a perfect, pretty heart, the lips below pink and tucked. His eyes went wide as she clambered onto the bed, straddling his face.

"Here, I have breakfast ready for you," she said.

Preston was certain this was another feint, just one more tease meant to wind him up and deny him. Then Lady Khan's warm pussy pressed against his mouth and he realized he didn't know anything at all.

He licked up her lips, head spinning. As he'd confessed to Miss Ying and Miss Grace, he'd only been to third base with four women, and the last had been long enough ago that he was nervous to suddenly have a pussy pressed to his face. He lapped, wildly, tongue whipping every which way.

"Slow down there, Tiger," Lady Khan said. "Long, slow licks. Go ahead."

Preston did as he was told, trying to calm his racing heartbeat and make sure each lick went all the way up her wetness. She tasted almost like roasting coffee, the flavor strong and absorbing. He licked again and again, waiting for her to tell him what to do next.

"My, my. You're nervous. I heard you hadn't done this sort of thing much, but I'll give you credit–you *are* eager," said Lady Khan.

She lifted herself off his face, sitting back on Preston's chest. He tried to crane his neck forward to touch her again but couldn't reach. The mistress curled her lips to the side in a smile.

"Very eager. I like that." She pressed her hips forward. "Come on, come and get it."

Preston pushed his head forward, still inches away from Lady Khan's crotch. He stretched his tongue out in hopes he could close the gap, but no matter how he tried, he couldn't reach her. Desperation flooded Preston and he felt himself grow stiff against the leather sleepsack. In a hopeless gambit, he started blowing warm air on the mistress's pussy, thinking it might delight her enough for her to bring her wetness back to his mouth.

Lady Khan tsk tsked.

"Is that the best you can do?" she teased.

It wasn't. Preston craned his neck even further, making his face go beet red and cutting off his oxygen, all to gain a measly sliver of an inch that still left him much too far away from her. Pent-up and frustrated, Preston grunted angrily, trying to pull his body up against the confining sleepsack and the weight of Lady Khan on his chest. She grinned down at him. Clearly she was enjoying the sight of his struggle.

"Don't worry," she said. "You'll have plenty of time to practice this morning."

Preston's gaze darted up to her, hope in his eyes.

Lady Khan barked a laugh. "Oh, not on me," she said. "After you said how few partners you had, we figured we'd do you a favor and send you to cunnilingus training today. I think you'll find it… educational."

With that, Lady Khan whipped the hem of her robe over Preston's head, tenting his view so that all he could see was her pussy and her heart-shaped patch of pubic hair. She slipped a hand under her robe and began to play with her clit, making a V with her fingers to rub it in slow, lazy circles. With her robe over his head, the roasted coffee smell of her became thick and mouth-coating. He closed his eyes and breathed her in, up until the point that she came in a throaty, moaning orgasm. She caught her breath and Preston hoped he would never have to stop smelling her.

A LESSON IN PEARL DIVING

Unlike the day before, Preston was not escorted to his next destination. Instead, after Lady Khan had unzipped Preston and let him shower again before changing into an embarrassingly short hemmed, almost skimpy terry cloth robe and a pair of too-small slippers. He has also been given a floor to go to and a room to navigate to: 9th floor, C Suite.

By the time he was done with his shower, Lady Khan was gone, as was the leather sleepsack. The only thing that remained was a folded up napkin that read, "Smell me."

Preston was unsurprised to find the napkin smelled like her pussy.

He wandered out of the room in a daze. It was strange to be allowed to move about the Silk Dungeon freely, and although thoughts of snooping where he shouldn't popped into the back of Preston's mind, he didn't hold onto them for long. He had been given a responsibility to escort himself–a privilege, really–and he didn't want to let the mistress who'd given him that privilege down.

As Preston rode the elevator down, another thought popped into his head: A rat in a maze, looking for cheese.

The 9th floor had a cold and sterile feel, reminding Preston of a hospital wing. Bright fluorescents flickered overhead and emitted a low buzz that wormed its way into his ears. His slippers shuffled on the coated rubber hallway flooring. As he passed by rooms–the light wood doors also looking like they'd fit right in at a medical ward–he saw their observation windows were blocked out from the inside. He was so very tempted to push one of these doors open and see what was inside, but resisted the urge, continuing to scan the room placards to find the one labeled "C Suite".

At the very end of the hallway, Preston saw a pair of double doors. That had to be the room he was looking for. As he got closer, he heard the sounds of sultry, erotic moaning, the noise of a woman nearing orgasm. The closer he got to the double doors the closer the mystery woman seemed to get to cumming and by the time he was ready to push the door open, she was screaming with ecstasy.

Preston opened the double doors.

A dark, open space awaited him. There were standing screens, with projects that cast movies onto them and onto the walls behind, a dizzying collection of clips of faces pressed up against feminine crotches, tongues swirling and lapping and licking, noses pushed against swollen clits, mouths glistening with gushed wetness. The audio cut from the screaming orgasm to another woman's joy, and looking around Preston connected the timing with one of the clips of a creamed black dildo being shoved deep into an Asian pussy projected to be the size of the wall. Underneath the audio was a thumping bass track that Preston felt deep in his bones.

It was like a scene out of A Clockwork Orange, only with videos of women receiving body-quaking oral pleasure. Simply watching the clips and listening to the nonstop switching audio tracks made Preston hard.

He saw the contraption set up in the middle of the room.

There was a padded kneeler, like in a confessional, set with two divots on either end that was placed between a standing wooden metal post in the front and a low table behind; on the table was a pair of leather sleeves joined together, adorned with a column of gleaming metal buckles. Preston looked closer. He saw the metal post in front had something attached to it–a flesh-toned silicone replica of a pussy.

"Miss Ying told me you've only fucked four girls," a female voice said.

Preston spun around. Then he saw the woman who had been hiding in the shadows of C Suite. She was petite and sinewy under her skintight crimson leather bodysuit, her hair shaved down on one side, the other side styled to fall over her face in a severe slash, with dyed red highlights. There was a row of piercings along the ear on the shaved side of her head, as well as a lip ring and a dermal in her chin. Contacts gave the tanned Asian woman unnaturally gray eyes that looked haunting in the dark of the room.

"No wonder why you suck at eating pussy," she said. "I had went down on more girls than that before I had graduated from high school. But don't worry, I'm going to give you a crash course in pearl diving."

The woman flicked her tongue out and Preston saw there were three silver studs down the middle. She pressed a button on a small remote she was holding and all at once the screens changed to an identical titlecard with words in a playful, color font and a cartoon illustration of an oyster with a pearl inside that looked more than subtly sexual. The title read: "Pearl Diving with Daddy Dong".

Preston couldn't help but give her a puzzled look. She was ready for it.

"I always hated my last name when I was growing up," the mistress–Daddy Dong, apparently–explained. "Dong. You know the jokes I had to hear?"

As she spoke, Daddy Dong urged Preston to take off his robe and slippers and guided him to the contraption in the center of the room, pushing him down to rest his knees in the divots of the kneeler. She moved his arms behind his back, putting them loosely into the leather sleeves.

"It only got worse when I realized I liked girls. Boys can be such assholes, saying the worst shit behind your back. 'She wants to give those girls the Dong', 'At least there's one Dong between them', 'Bet she wishes she had a real Dong'. Always the same, lame jokes, again and again."

Daddy Dong tightened the conjoined leather sleeves, pulling Preston's arms together behind his back. Each belt pulled and buckle secured made his shoulders roll back and his chest puff out. His mounting helplessness was made worse when the mistress strapped down his bent legs and pushed him forwards, towards the silicone pussy. She picked up a leather belt attached by a lead to the front post that Preston hadn't noticed before and wrapped it around his waist, fastening it. This left Preston in a leaning forward, kneeling position, the fake pussy shoved in his face.

"But I learned to own what made me feel small," said Daddy Dong with pride. "I started calling myself 'The Dong', taking the wind out of the sails of the guys who tried to make fun of me. I stopped trying to be the girly girl I wasn't and started showing up those same guys in sports and being crass and even picking up pussy. A lot of them hated me. Some of them became friends. But they *all* learned to respect me."

Preston jumped as the mistress reached between his legs.

"Relax," Daddy Dong said. "I just need to make sure you have the proper motivation for our lesson."

At first, Preston thought she was going to stroke him off and just as he was beginning to feel bad about the idea of a lesbian dominatrix pleasuring a man, he realized she had a different kind of motivation in mind. He felt her attach a rubber ring around the base of his cock and balls and looked down to see red and black snaking out from the rubber ring. He followed it as much as he could, and saw it led to a black box tucked under the padded kneeler.

"Watch the video," said Daddy Dong, pressing a button on her small remote.

The screens switched to a slow, steady video of a white woman kneeling between an Asian girl's legs. There was a close up of the woman's pink tongue licking up the shaved lips and up to the rosy, hard clit.

"Do what you see on screen," the mistress commanded.

To get Preston moved, Daddy Dong pressed the remote and he felt a jolting shock in his balls. He tried to jump, but the straps, armbinders, and belt kept him in place.

"Lick for Daddy," said Daddy Dong. "Or else you get the shock again."

With his eyes on the projector screen set up right behind the wooden post, Preston mimicked the white girl's licking. He ran his tongue up the silicone pussy, trying not to feel silly. As he did he felt something else–a slight tingling in his balls and cock that was much softer than the jolt before, the little pulse of electricity making him thrum with excitement. When he lifted his tongue off the fake pussy, the buzzing went away, starting again when his tongue touched it once more.

Preston's engineer brain figured it out right away. Every time he touched the silicone with his tongue, he was completing a circuit with the ring the mistress had put on the base of his cock and balls, one that sent a pleasurable tingle of electricity up his shaft. He licked again, as slow as the woman on screen, enjoying how the light *thump-thump-thump* ran up to his swollen cockhead.

"That's right. Lick just like the video shows you and you get rewarded," said Daddy Dong.

After a few minutes of Preston repeating the same licking motion as demonstrated on screen, the petite mistress stepped around to the front of the contraption, blocking the video. The pussy-on-the-post was exactly as high up as Daddy Dong's own crotch, making Preston almost believe he was licking her. She pressed the remote, changing all the other screens back to the assortment of pussy licking videos, and now Preston was forced to lick the silicone slit from memory, using the rhythmic feel of the electricity on his genitals for guidance.

The moans and sighs from the other videos started to distract Preston. He struggled to find the rhythm again and as his licking got sloppy, he felt a painful burst of electricity in his balls. He jumped, yelping out loud.

"Focus," warned Daddy Dong. "Lick. Lick, Lick."

Her words were a metronome meant to recenter him and he licked along to them, the tingling, teasing electricity resuming.

"Women aren't like men. They don't just want it faster and faster and faster until they pop. They want it slow. Steady. A reliable, unceasing beat of pleasure that they can ride to the heights of orgasmic bliss. Yes, there comes a time when you're worshipping a woman that you need to be more intense, but you don't start there. You have to *earn* it. Keep going. You'll know when you've earned it."

Preston kept licking, Daddy Dong going quiet so that he was forced to find the rhythm on his own through the chaotic noise all around. When he failed, he received a nasty shock–shocks that Daddy Dong made Preston find his own way through, teaching him to create his own rhythm. A minute of licking turned to two, then five, then ten, and Preston's jaw began to feel like it was on fire. He was making more mistakes now and receiving more shocks. When he thought he could take no more, Daddy Dong stepped to the side, allowing Preston to watch the demonstration video again. It was easier to draw his tongue up along the silicone pussy with the visual aid, but it did nothing to relieve his aching jaw and tongue.

After more than twenty minutes of nonstop licking, Daddy Dong clicked the remote. The screens went back to the "Pearl Diving with Daddy Dong" titlecard and the electricity turned off.

"Very good," she said to him. "Let me see your tongue."

Preston held out his tongue obediently. It was heavy and sore and dry. The mistress snatched it in her fingers, pressing her thumb and forefinger against the tired flesh.

"Thank me for what I've shown you so far," she said.

"Thanf thuu," Preston managed.

Daddy Dong gathered up a mouthful of spit and dangled out a heavy dollop between her pierced lips, letting it slowly drop onto Preston's tongue. The spit was warm and soothing. She let go of his tongue and Preston brought her spit into his mouth, savoring the salve.

"You can't always be moving just your tongue," she told him. "Do that and your jaw is going to cramp up and you're barely going to be able to last five minutes without being in agony. You have to move your head too, letting the muscles in your neck do some work."

She held the flat of her palm out towards Preston.

"Go ahead, try it," she said.

Preston stuck his tongue back out and tried using his neck instead of his jaw. The mistress was right, it *was* a lot easier. He licked along the crevices of her palm, tasting whatever patchouli fragrance she had on. She pulled her hand away.

"Now, along with rhythm, you need to learn how to delight. A tongue licking in a straight line up a woman's lips is fine, but I teach my 'students' to do better. Watch the video."

On the screens, there was now a letter shown in the upper corner of the screen, followed by the white woman licking the glistening Asian pussy in front of her. An "A", followed by two slants licks up and one across, a "B", followed by a lick up and a 3-shaped lick down, a "C", followed by an arching lick down from the clit to the base of the Asian girl's pussy.

It was the alphabet. The white woman was licking with alphabet shapes.

The alphabet continued, with some really exotic licks for the more complicated, like "G", and "M", and "Q". Once the wet pussy had had the entire alphabet licked across it, the video looped over.

"Once you've learned to keep a rhythm, you can vary how you lick. That variation keeps the woman you're worshipping from getting distracted by your incompetence or even worse, bored. Combining neck movements with spelling out the alphabet takes a little bit of practice, but lucky for you, we have plenty of time."

Daddy Dong pointed to the silicone pussy that Preston was getting very, very familiar with. She clicked her remote and Preston felt a small shock.

"Get to it," she ordered.

This exercise was much harder than the first, and to Preston's relief there were no shocks when he messed up. Not at first, anyway. Once he had stumbled his way through the whole alphabet twice, giving the fake pussy in front of him fifty adoring licks, the pleasant, rewarding electric tingles and punishing shocks began again. The shocks were stronger now too, though not always, making it so that each time Preston felt one he wouldn't know if it would be a mild annoyance or a sudden burst of pain in his balls. Daddy Dong switched all but the screen in front of Preston to the chaotic mash of porn videos and walked around the contraption he was fastened to, blocking the screen with each circuit. Sometimes she passed quickly, other times she moved painstakingly slowly, forcing Preston to keep up with which letter was next.

"A, B, C, D, E, F, G…" she started to sing, throwing off Preston's concentration. He jolted from another shock, a mean one this time. He flailed against his bindings in frustration. "…H, I, J, K, L-M-N-O-P…"

Preston messed up again. Another strong shock. He grunted in pain, but didn't dare stop licking.

"Q, R, S, T, U, V…" Daddy Dong was just about to cross in front of the screen but turned around and started the other way. Preston stared at the screen unblinking, licking to its steady parade of letter instructions. "...W, Y, X, and Z..."

The mistress in the crimson bodysuit stopped in front of the screen, totally blocking Preston's view. "Now I know my ABCs, next time won't you lick with me."

Without being able to see the screen, Preston hopelessly tried to find his place, messing up again and again. The shocks were unpredictable and he kept bracing himself for a big one, flinching and jumping as electricity zapped his balls.

"Lost?" taunted Daddy Dong. "If you just keep licking the same letter, you'll get it eventually. The worst that'll happen is that you'll be shocked 25 times..."

She swayed back and forth, but never enough to move out of the way for Preston to see the screen. He grunted in pain and then gave a whimpering cry, so frustrated that he couldn't find his place. After a dozen shocks, Daddy Dong moved to the side, letting him resume his licking. He spelled the alphabet out on the fake pussy two more whole times before she stopped the electricity and flashed the screens back to the titlecard.

"Rhythm. Delightful variation. That's an excellent start," said Daddy Dong. "And if you do a good job, you'll get that pussy nice and wet and wanting. Think of it like knocking on a door for just a bit too long. You want her *excited*, wondering when the fuck you're finally going to give her clit some attention. You'll know she's ready when she starts to seem impatient. That's when you go for the pearl."

Daddy Dong clicked the remote and all the screens continued the demonstration from before. This time the white woman was up at the top of the Asian girl's pussy, tongue stretched towards the swollen, pink pearl of her clit. She brought her tongue across it, side to side, several times. Then she switched to a circular motion and then an up and down licking motion. Each time there was a clear pause between these motions.

"The clit is like a lock," explained Daddy Dong. "You need to find the right 'key' for the pussy you're licking. Side-to-side, swirls, and up-and-down are the most likely keys, and you have to go light with them at first, otherwise you'll ruin the mood. Imagine a lockpick–force it and it'll break off. Go light until you find what works. Give it a try."

Following along to the video, Preston licked side to side, in a swirling motion, up and down. He repeated these motions a half-dozen times, the electricity turned off while he figured out the basic moves. Daddy Dong clicked the remote and continued her explanation. The video switched to the white woman swirling her tongue around the Asian girl's clit.

"Once you've found the key though, you *stay repetitive*. This is not the time to be creative. This is where she'll be grinding her hips into your face, gripping onto your hair, and moaning and crying so loud that you'll be sure the people next door can hear. This is also where you DON'T DARE FUCKING STOP." Daddy Dong's shouting words startled Preston. She stared sternly at him. "I'm absolutely serious. Don't stop. Don't speed up. Don't change what you're doing. You keep at it unerringly, until she cums. This is why it's important to learn to use your neck. If you burn out because your jaw hurts, you will have ruined all your hard work."

Daddy Dong patted the top of the metal post, guiding Preston back to his tongue-exhausting work. Even with his neck motions, he was still plenty achy and he wondered if his licking regimen would ever stop. He moved to the silicone pussy's clit and dragged his tongue around it at the same speed of the video on the screen in front of him. Instantly he was rewarded with a delightful electric buzzing up his cock.

"Remember, stay with it and don't stop," warned Daddy Dong.

Another click of the remote, another change of all the other screens except the one in front of him to a collage of frenzied porn. Preston kept his eyes trained on the screen in front of him, soon feeling the burn in his tongue as he went around and around and around. He idly wondered how long he'd been here for. Half an hour? Forty-five minutes? Longer?

The fake pussy began to vibrate and Preston was so surprised that he stopped licking it. For his curiosity, he received a painful shock to his balls and went back to licking. The pussy was no longer vibrating.

"You stop, then you start all over again," Daddy Dong said.

It took Preston another few minutes of licking before the pussy began vibrating again. He pushed past his surprise and continued swirling his tongue around the silicone clit, the stereo sound moans all around him spurring him on, even if they were synced to the other videos. The vibrating became more intense and then something really unexpected happened–Preston got a shock to his balls.

"Fuck," he grunted, caught totally by surprise. What was that? He hadn't done anything wrong.

"You need to be prepared for the unexpected," said Daddy Dong, having manually shocked him. "She might claw your back or crush your head in her thighs or, if she's like what some of the mistresses here at the Dungeon enjoy, actually shock your balls. You need to be able to keep going." She pointed a finger towards the pussy, its glossy black nail reflecting the demonstration video in front of Preston.

Still feeling the burn in his balls and the ache in his tongue, Preston started from scratch. Five minutes of licking and the pussy was vibrating, another five minutes and there was the first shock to Preston's balls. He faltered for a second but quickly resumed his swirling, worshiping licks.

"Good," Daddy Dong said.

Her praise washed over Preston, encouraging him.

Soon the shocks were coming every thirty seconds, the fake pussy vibrating so much it was getting hard to keep his swirls on its faux clit. Preston fought through the disorientation and the pain. He was sure he had to be close. The shocks went down to every fifteen seconds, then ten, and by the time the fake pussy was vibrating wildly in its metal pole casing, there was just one awful, agonizing, long shock to Preston's tortured balls. But he was determined not to quit. He swirled his tongue over and over and over and over and over, feeling like he was going to lose his mind, and it was right when he was at his breaking point, thinking he could take no more, that he was rewarded with the shocks stopping and all of the video screens switching to a close up shot to show for the first time the Asian girl's face as she cried in joy at her out of control orgasm.

The pussy's vibrating quieted and Preston was left panting for breath. He was so tired he didn't even care that he rested his head against the metal pole to help him catch his breath, realizing then he was beyond hard, his cock jutting up deliriously from his legs. He felt Daddy Dong's cool hand on his sweaty back.

"Good job," said Daddy Dong. But her praise was quickly tempered when she added: "You now have the pussy eating skills of a clumsy high school dyke. I think you've earned some breakfast."

As soon as she said the words, Preston realized how hungry he was. The mistress undid his bindings–the belt, the straps, the armbinders that had left Preston's hands numb–and helped him to his feet. He was shaking and didn't think he'd ever be able to speak again. She draped his robe around him and steadied him as he put his slippers back on. She clicked the remote twice. The sound in the room muted and then there was a knock at the door.

"Come in," said Daddy Dong.

The suite door opened, casting harsh yellow light into the dark space. Preston saw the silhouette of the female waitress from last night, the one who had served him and Mistress Midori the steak.

"She'll take you to breakfast," Daddy Dong said, patting him on the shoulder.

Preston stepped away, shakily.

"Preston," the mistress said.

He turned, thinking she was about to offer him one last accolade for his tongue-numbing work.

Instead she said: "Remember, don't you dare fucking stop."

"Yeth, thanf thuu," said Preston, his tongue too swollen and tired to speak straight.

BREAKFAST OF CHAMPIONS

Preston shuffled behind the female waiter. She was dressed in a fitted, pristine tuxedo that showed off her slender frame. She said nothing to Preston, leading him wordlessly to the 9th floor elevator. He had a strong suspicion she was not one of the Silk Dungeon's mistresses.

"Can I ask you a question?" he said, as she pressed the button for the 11th floor. So, as he guessed–he was going back to Mistress Midori's room. His tongue still hurt.

"I don't know, can you?" the female waiter asked back in heavily Japanese-accented English.

Hah. Touche, thought Preston. He decided to press his luck.

"Do you work for the Silk Dungeon? I kind of thought, you know… it would just be some dominatrixes here in a bunch of kinky rooms or something. But it seems bigger than that."

The woman smiled tightly. She chose her words carefully, either due to her English or to make an exact point: "The Silk Dungeon is many things. Do not mistake a tree for a forest."

The profundity of her response–grammatical error aside–made Preston pause. He had come to the Silk Dungeon longing for an adventure, but he'd be lying if he wasn't also expecting the place to fit in a neat, little tidy box as a kind of BDSM fetish amusement park for people who could afford the price of admission. Between what he'd seen so far, what Lady Khan had told him about himself, and even this offhand remark from someone Preston was ready to dismiss as no higher than his tech company's janitorial staff, maybe he was wrong.

The elevator opened at the 11th floor and the female waiter pushed her way out first, making Preston follow behind. They returned to room 1119. The woman gestured towards the door, not even opening it up for him.

"In here," she said.

When his hand touched the doorknob, she cleared her throat, drawing his attention. Preston looked over, waiting for her to say whatever was clearly on her mind.

"Yes?" he said, a little irritated when she didn't immediately share her thoughts.

She gave another tight smile. Then she spoke quietly, not wanting anyone else to hear: "You come here and you think this world is built for you," she said, tripping over her English. "You think we wait, for you. But we don't need you. You need us."

Before Preston could process her words, the female waiter reached over and opened the door for Preston, pretty much forcing him to go inside without responding. Once he was through the doorway, she pulled the door shut.

The room was not the same as it had been yesterday. There was no longer any table on wheels nor a pair of chairs, one with cuffs, and there wasn't even the same bed anymore. Instead, in the night the entire room had been refitted, its former carpeting gone in favor of tatami panels, its bed now a futon on the floor, its table now one of those low Japanese style ones where you had to sit crossed legged. Mistress Midori was seated at the low table, wearing a green silk kimono with a tall, wide white obi belt. Her hair was up in a bun, held that way with a wooden ornament that had a string of beads hanging from it that tinkled gently as she moved her head. She smiled at Preston.

"Have a seat," she said.

Preston sat down, his arms still stiff from the binders. In front of him was a closed bento box. Mistress Midori had a similar one. He looked at his bento with cautious optimism. Mistress Midori poured him some hot green tea.

"Did you sleep okay?" she asked.

Preston nodded. "As good as I could…" he said.

Mistress Midori opened her bento. Inside were a selection of colorful breakfast tarts, both sweet and savory. She popped one in her mouth and chewed happily.

"We debated how to keep you overnight. Under a bed, in a cage, maybe strapped to a hospital gurney, naked. But I loved the idea of the sleepsack. Confinement and closeness, yet not being able to do anything about it. It's poetic."

The mistress looked at Preston to open his bento. He lifted the lid and saw his own selection of breakfast tarts, relieved the bento wasn't left empty as some trick. Then, as he looked closer he saw his tarts were different from the mistress's. They were specially shaped to look like tiny little pussies.

No doubt it had a grueling effort to shape the breakfast pastries this way, though all Preston could think of was his "pearl diving" training with Daddy Dong.

"Show me what you learned," crooned Mistress Midori.

Preston took a nervous sip of his green tea. "Really?" he asked.

Mistress Midori's expression hardened. "Just because I allow you to dine with me, doesn't mean you're allowed to disrespect me," she said, her voice darkening as she spoke. "I'm not going to ask you twice."

Preston picked up one of the tarts, a pale pussy-shaped one that was dusted with sugar. He licked the top of it for Mistress Midori to see. Had he not just spent over an hour being drilled on cunnilingus, his embarrassment would've gotten the better of him, but after the training it was only too natural for Preston to lick the pussy pastry to his own imaginary beat. As he did, he tasted the insides–sweet strawberry cream–and found himself both hungry and horny. After a minute of licking, he started drawing the alphabet on the pastry; the mistress stopped him.

"That's enough," she said. "You can eat. Just make sure you give each tart a little attention before you have it."

The two ate quietly as Preston licked his way through the pastries. They were magnificent, and not simply because he was starving. There was strawberry creme and cheese custard and chocolate and ham with egg and tomato basil and more, all with the distinct Japanese quality of being flavorful without being too sweet or cloying. Whenever Preston's teacup neared empty, Mistress Midori refilled it for him with a geisha-like awareness.

Noticing him watching her practiced moments, Mistress Midori said: "The Lotus Experience package we have has an entire geisha sequence where the client roleplays as a traveler in a foreign land, charmed by a trio of geishas–only for them to decide that he's never going home and is going to stay in their tea house as their plaything. It's *very* sensual."

As the mistress spoke, her kimono slipped open. It seemed accidental but had to have been planned, thought Preston. It was open just enough for him to see deep into the mistress's cleavage and almost catch sight of her nipple. His cock poked towards the underside of the low lacquered table as he thought about it, averting his eyes back down to what remained of his pussy-shaped breakfast tarts.

"Are the packages and experiences the same for everyone?" Preston asked, genuinely curious.

The mistress left her kimono parted loosely in the front. "There are modular pieces, things we repurpose. It's never exactly the same of course, but why let a perfectly good idea go to waste? But the more intricate the package, the most bespoke it is–whatever is required to create the change we wish to see."

The change. What did that mean? Preston thought about what the female waiter had said about mistaking the forest for the trees. He picked up another tart, not even thinking as he lavished it with lewd oral attention, his tongue dipping between the pastry folds to taste the blackberry jam inside.

"What change are you trying to create with me?" asked Preston.

Mistress Midori paused. "The change you need in your life," she said.

Preston huffed a laugh. "Come on…"

"Do you really think I'm going to tell you?" asked the mistress. "And would you really want to know?"

Preston looked down, seeing that he had finished off the last of his bento breakfast. He took a sip of tea, emptying his cup as well. Mistress Midori did not refill it.

"I guess not," he said with a shrug.

"Time for a little dessert," Mistress Midori said.

Preston wanted to say, "Who has dessert with breakfast?" but he noticed there was nothing left on the table to have and no sign from the mistress that she was summoning the waiter to bring more food. He looked around, confused.

Mistress Midori stirred, putting her hands on the tatami behind her and leaning back slightly. Preston could hear the rustle of silk under the table and realized she was spreading her legs open. He glanced at her, seeking confirmation, and the knowing look in her eyes told him everything he needed to know: his dessert was between her legs.

As if in a trance, Preston slid his legs out from under the table and lowered himself to his belly so that he could fit underneath. He saw the green silk hanging over Mistress Midori's spread knees and down her creamy legs he saw the dark patch of her pubic hair. Without room to even get up on his hands and knees, Preston had to wiggle himself towards her, half-expecting her to pull herself away or push him to the side any second. She didn't. He inches closer so that his face was brushing up against her silky hair. He reached out his tongue to touch her.

After his time with the silicone pussy, he had forgotten how warm and soft the real thing was. He licked her slowly, with great big puppy-tongue licks as he settled into his "dessert". Mistress Midori shifted her hips, angling herself better to him, and Preston's simple licks soon gave way to the alphabet variations, the man licking his way from A to Z over and over as the mistress wetness rolled down his face, slicking his lips. She had a subtle musky scent of crushed petals to her and Preston thought just how different it was from the brief taste he'd gotten of Lady Khan. Mistress Midori rocked her hips against him as he moved his tongue along her, her silky black hair tickling his nose. The kimono tenting him between her legs made him soon feel hot and dazed, like Preston was living out some wet dream.

Above the table, the mistress was moaning. Preston remembered what Daddy Dong had said–think about knocking on a door for just a little too long, getting her impatient and wanting. He ran through the alphabet again, then settled on the letters that seemed to make Mistress Midori moan the loudest, "A", "J", "S", "W". Her rocking became more insistent and Preston had to time his licking to "ride" her grinding, grateful that he was using his neck as much as his jaw to lick the mistress's pussy. A few times he bonked his head on the underside of the table through the silk kimono, but he recovered quickly, not daring to break his rhythm.

Mistress Midori reached a hand under the table and pushed Preston's head up angrily towards her clit. She was ready. He reached for her pearl, licking up and down, in a swirl, and then side to side, the last motion making the mistress erupt in an overjoyed cry of bliss. That was the one. Preston licked side to side, moving his head back and forth like he was saying "no", finding the pace that made Mistress Midori's body tense up and her clawed grip on his head get even tighter. He kept his licking as steady and constant as he could, the crushed petal taste of her getting thicker and richer. Mistress Midori's deep moans filled the room. Preston had no idea how close she was but knew that whether it was five minutes or fifty, he couldn't screw things up now. He had to keep going.

With his face pressed to the Japanese pussy in front of him, Preston lost track of time. He felt like he'd been licking all day, like nothing else in the world mattered or existed. His entire universe was licking back and forth, back and forth, not caring that his face was covered in the mistress's wetness or it was so warm down under the table and between the mistress's legs that he thought he might pass out. So be it. If he passed out worshiping Mistress Midori, it would be a hell of a lot better than giving into fatigue and slowing his tonguing adoration.

The mistress's thighs tightened around Preston's face and with a deep, long groan, she came. Her body shook uncontrollably as she creamed his face, the gush of her wetness stunning Preston. He continued licking side-to-side until Mistress Midori inched him away–still buried between her legs, just with his tongue on her lips and not clit–and Preston lapped at her cream, not knowing having been prepared for this by Daddy Dong. He kept his licks light and slow and eventually the mistress's trembling quieted. She relaxed, leaving Preston under the table as she withdrew her legs, shifting so that one foot was on the tatami and the other was splayed out, her kimono hanging to just reveal her glistening muff.

"I see Dong's still an excellent teacher," said Mistress Midori after catching her breath. "You can come out now."

Preston wiggled out backwards, his robe riding up awkwardly; surely Mistress Midori got a kick out of the disheveled sight of him, especially after he'd just worked so hard to please her. He sat back down and though he was grateful to feel the room's cool air, his vision was still swimming. Through the spinning haze, he saw the mistress smiling at him.

"I hope you had enough to eat," teased Mistress Midori. "Because it's just about time for your next session."

PRINCESS YEONA

Mistress Midori took her phone out from inside her obi belt. She swiped it open and made a call.

"Yes. It's me. We're all done here. You can come get him. Great, see you soon."

She ended the call and put her phone face down on the low table.

"What have you learned about yourself so far?" the mistress asked Preston.

The suddenness of the question and knowing that someone was coming for him made Preston freeze up. His mind was blank.

"I, uh… I don't know," he said.

Mistress Midori scoffed. "You haven't learned a single thing about yourself so far?"

Preston glanced towards the door, expecting a knock any second.

"No, I, um, I'm sure I have," stammered Preston.

"Yet you can't think of a single thing," said Mistress Midori.

Preston strained his brain, digging for anything he might be able to share with the mistress. He didn't want the knock on the door to come before he'd answered her and so he searched for the first bit of self-discovery he could find. But it wasn't the first thing he wanted to share with her–or with anyone.

"Okay, I… I'm not as great as I thought I was," he said.

The mistress couldn't contain her laughter. "Modest, aren't we?"

"No, I mean, like… obviously you know my background, my job, my company. I've lived with all that for so long that it's become, like, I don't know… a kind of myth, you know? The myth of my success."

Mistress Midori listened attentively, giving Preston plenty of space to continue.

"I guess when you tell yourself a story enough times, it starts to become true to you," he continued. "And for me, I started to feel… brilliant. Like really brilliant, a top tier mind, a scion of knowledge and confidence. Unbreakable, in a way. I came here partly because it seemed like the opposite of who I was. You know? Being told what to do instead of telling people what to do, all that stuff. But now… my myth, my story… I can see the fiction very, very clearly."

"What about your time here has made you think this way?" asked Mistress Midori, speaking to Preston with the calm of a psychoanalyst.

"Honestly… I don't know. I mean, everything, kinda," Preston said.

Mistress Midori stayed quiet and Preston felt the pressure to be more specific. He sighed.

"Okay. Don't take this the wrong way or anything, but you–and the other women here, the mistresses–aren't what I expected."

"What did you expect?" Mistress Midori asked him.

"I guess, you know. S-sex workers? Like, escorts but with more theater and spectacle." Preston chewed his lower lip and quickly added, "I'm sorry if that's offensive."

Mistress Midori ignored the apology. "How have you found us to be instead?" she asked.

Preston took a deep breath. "In control. Does that make sense? Like, in my mind I think of escorts and stuff as women trying to make their, uh, clients happy. But the mistresses here, they, well… obviously they're in control, that's kind of the whole point, but it's like they would be in control even if we weren't here. Like, if I saw you or the others on the street, it's like the dynamic between us would still exist. Am I making any sense here?"

Mistress Midori pursed her lips. "You've been well-off for a long time, Preston. Is that right?"

Preston nodded.

"When was the last time you couldn't buy something you wanted? Within reason, obviously."

Preston shrugged and said, "My late 20s, maybe? That's the last time I remember looking at people in first class and being jealous."

"Jealous. Now there's an interesting word," said Mistress Midori.

"How so?" asked Preston.

There was a knock on the door. Preston's time was up.

"One moment," Mistress Midori called to whoever was waiting on the other side of the door. She turned back to Preston. "A round peg can fill a square hole, but it doesn't mean it's the right fit."

More riddles, thought Preston. He looked at her blankly. "And…?"

The mistress smiled, looking like she enjoyed knowing something Preston did not.

"And perhaps you're beginning to realize your hole isn't quite as filled as you thought," she said.

The double entendre wasn't lost on Preston, especially after having to wear the puppy tail butt plug yesterday. But what hole was she really talking about? How was he supposed to fill it? And what did jealousy have to do with it?

Mistress Midori called towards the door again.

"You can come in now," she said.

The door swung open and Preston realized Mistress Midori had chosen her words carefully. Standing there was a Korean woman in an eye-popping, extravagant outfit made of shiny black latex and gleaming silver accents. The top had short shoulder sleeves, with a heart-shaped cutout above the bust and countless silver spikes around the cup of the woman's breasts. A reflective silver collar was clasped around her neck. The bottom half was a pair of latex leggings that conformed to the Korean woman's long, thin legs, with silver stud piping down the sides. She wore shiny boots with a tall, chunky heel. The same spikes that were along the woman's bust were across the tops of her boots.

But Preston couldn't bring himself to look at the most eye-popping part of her outfit. Not yet.

Instead he brought his gaze up to her round babyface. Her lips were blush pink, her smoky eyeshadow making her eyes look even more monolidded than they were. The woman's hair was cut into a soft bob with angled bangs that just missed covering her left eye and her smile had a sweet, pillowy plushness to it.

He looked down.

There it was. More than seven inches of thick, veiny, shiny, latex cock jutting from the woman's crotch.

"Preston, this is the Silk Dungeon's very own princess, Princess Yeona. Yeona, meet Preston." Mistress Midori pronounced the "princess's" name like *yo-na*, the "e" almost silent.

"Hiiiii!" she exclaimed, waving excitedly. As she did, the phallus jutting out from her crotch bobbed back and forth.

Preston stared speechless at the Korean woman.

"Well, don't be rude," chided Mistress Midori. "Say hi."

"Hi," Preston eked out.

"No, not like that," said Mistress Midori. "She's a princess. You have to say: Hi, Princess."

"Hi, Princess," repeated Preston.

"Princess Yeona has been looking for her prince for a long, long time," said Mistress Midori. "You might be it. But first she has to see if you're the right fit. You know, like in Cinderella, when the prince goes around looking to see which foot the glass slipper fits on."

Princess Yeona giggled. "Oh yes. Something like that," she said.

"Go on," urged Mistress Midori. "You won't need that robe, either."

Preston stood up, numbly shedding his robe and slippers. Without her tall heels, Preston would've surely been taller than Princess Yeona, but with them on she was half a head taller than him. She put her arm around him and pulled him close so that he could feel the mild bite of the silver spikes around her breasts, along with the smooth latex.

"Right this way," she said, ushering Preston out of the room.

Princess Yeona's chunky heels thumped on the hallways carpeting. She walked with an energetic gait, latex-clad body swaying against Preston's.

"I'm suuuuper excited to get to play with you," she said. "We're going to have so much fun!"

Preston swallowed hard, his throat feeling dry. He could still taste Mistress Midori's pussy on his tongue. Somehow he didn't think more pussy was in his future any time soon. They got onto the elevator and the Princess hit the button for the 7th floor.

"How many floors does the Silk Dungeon have, anyway?" asked Preston, wondering if Princess Yeona's bubbly demeanor might make her more forthcoming than some of the other mistresses.

But she answered him just as cryptically as the rest: "As many as we need."

The elevator doors opened on the 7th floor. Preston was met with a sprawl of sultry color, with blue and pink bulbs illuminating the dark, shadowy hallway. On the wall were neon signs in English, Korean, Japanese, Chinese, and other languages he couldn't figure out. Some seemed like advertisements for beers or karaoke, while others were more mysterious. Long, hanging curtains covered the doorways, all with a slit down the middle, like those Preston had seen for Japanese sushi dens. He tried to look through those narrow slits to see what was hiding beyond the curtains, but it was too dark in the rooms and the blue and pink lights overhead too disorienting to get a good look.

They came to a hanging pink curtain with Korean characters on it in white.

"Can you guess what this says?" the Princess asked Preston.

"Princess Yeona?" he asked.

Princess Yeona clapped her hands together cheerfully. "That's right! Good job!"

The juxtaposition of the woman's sunny disposition and her severe spike-covered, latex outfit–and the dildo sticking out from her crotch–baffled Preston. If anything, he would've imagined that a dominatrix named "Daddy Dong" to be the one bearing a strap-on, not giving lessons in cunnilingus. The Silk Dungeon seemed full of these contradictions, maybe intentionally so to keep Preston and the rest of the men who entered on their toes.

Princess Yeona parted the hanging doorway curtain with the back of her hand. Preston stepped inside, heart beating hard. The only light in the room was from the thirty or forty tea candles spread throughout the space, some set up on standing candelabras, others on shelves, some positioned strategically next to some ominous and odd-looking item, casting it in mixed shadow and light. There was music playing from a retro radio made of chrome and pink metal. It was playing Korean pop music, one of those bouncy, techno-rap girl groups that had become so popular the last ten years. Princess Yeona hummed along to the music without even realizing it.

There were black silk tapestries on the wall with prints of delicate thin-stemmed flowers and tranquil gardens, with blocks of Korean lettering in each corner. Several small tables and end tables were spread strategically across the space, acting as constellations around the room's main attraction: a luxurious bed with a dark metal frame that was in the center of the room. The bedding was the same pink as the retro radio and Preston saw that on either end of the bed, where there would be the head and footboard, were instead pairs of stocks. Each had three holes to allow for plenty of configurations and from the look of the well-worn hinges, they had been used many, many times before.

Preston fidgeted anxiously.

"Don't be afraid," Princess Yeona whispered in his ear. "I'll be gentle." He was shocked when she ran her tongue up it and bolted up to a standing straight position.

The Princess sat Preston down on the edge of the bed, standing over him and seeming even more towering than before.

"This is your first time, right? I wouldn't count yesterday," she said.

Clearly she was talking about the plug without saying it. Preston nodded sheepishly. It started to set in–this Korean woman was going to fuck him with the strap-on.

"Well, it's a little early I suppose, but maybe this will help you relax…"

Princess Yeona reached towards one of the end tables, which Preston realized was actually a sleek minifridge. Its light was low, but he could still see rows of small bottles of Korean liquor inside. The Princess pulled out a green bottle with a decorative label and opened a drawer above the minifridge, retrieving two cups. All these she set down on a table next to the bed that she pulled over so that it was in front of Preston. She sat on the bed next to him, staying close enough so that he could feel the latex on his naked hip.

Princess Yeona cracked open the bottle and poured both of them a glass.

"As the princess here, you really should be pouring me," she said in a lecturer's drawl. "But you're okay for today." She held her cup up to Preston, encouraging him to do the same. "*Geonbae.* Cheers."

They clinked their ceramic cups and Preston took a sip. He'd had this liquor before–soju, he was pretty sure it was called–and drank down the semi-sweet, peachy liquid. He remembered hearing it was dangerously easy to drink and after downing most of his glass in one big sip, he could see why. Princess Yeona refilled his cup.

"Tell me about yourself," the Princess said. "What do you like to do for fun?"

"Fun," said Preston, feeling the liquor hit him already. He sipped from his refilled cup. "I don't know the last time I had fun."

Princess Yeona matched him sip for sip, showing off that legendary Korean drinking endurance Preston had also heard so much about. "That's so sad!" she said. "I know you work hard, but you really can't remember the last time you had fun? What about your stay here? Has that been fun?"

"Heh. I don't know if 'fun' is the word I would use," said Preston. He set his empty cup down and Princess Yeona was already refilling it before finishing off her own. Jesus, the woman could drink.

She looked at him with a faint crinkle of disappointment in her face. "You aren't having fun?"

"I'm enjoying it, I think. That's for sure," said Preston. The liquor loosened his tongue and between it and Princess Yeona's cheery style, he found it very easy to be honest with her. "But 'fun' feels like the wrong word. I don't know. Do you guys have fun being on the other side of it?"

Her lidded eyes flashed a fiery certainty. "Oh, yes. I have *soooo* much fun here. I get to learn about all kinds of people, I get to play games with them, I get to drink and invite boys to my room…"

Somehow Preston's cup was empty again and Princess Yeona was refilling it again. Just as he was thinking they were nearly done with the small bottle of soju, she was grabbing another, setting it on the table for when they were ready for it.

"This is your room?" asked Preston.

"You guessed it was my name on the curtain," the Princess said. "What else would it be?"

"You sleep here?"

Princess Yeona gave him a plush, sly smile. "We each have a few rooms here. Some are for sleep. Others are for… other things."

This time it was Princess Yeona who threw her cup back first, lapping Preston. He felt the pressure to keep up with her and then she was opening the second bottle and pouring them more.

"Whoa, whoa, I might need to slow down," said Preston, although he didn't mean it. Not really.

"Don't you know how it is in Korea?" asked the Princess. "When your cup is empty, you get refilled. If you don't want anymore, you stop drinking."

"It kind of feels like you're trying to get me drunk," said Preston, distantly amazed at how direct he was being. The soju wasn't just tasty, it was *strong*.

"You've never tried to get someone drunk so you can get them in bed?" Princess Yeona asked back. The innocent look she flashed him made her admission seem unreal.

"Uhhh, I'm not sure…" said Preston.

"There are lots of ways to have fun" said the Princess, going back to their other conversation. "Being someone's puppy can be fun. Sleeping in a leather bodybag can be fun. Getting fucked in the ass can be fun. It just depends on your state of mind."

Again, the Silk Dungeon had reared its strangely profound head. Preston certainly didn't think she was wrong–even if her telling him what she was going to do to him sent a slight chill down his spine.

"Does it hurt?" he asked.

"Having fun?" asked Princess Yeona with a teasing laugh.

"No, you know…" Preston looked between her legs at the latex strap-on.

The Princess hmmed. "Do spicy chicken wings hurt?"

"Hah. A little," said Preston.

"But people still eat them," she said. "Why do you think that is?"

Preston saw that this time it was Princess Yeona's cup that was empty. Emboldened by his buzz, he took the soju bottle and poured for her and then for himself. She gave him a wide, beaming smile.

"If I had to guess… it's because people find it exciting to feel a little hurt. A little thrill. Like on a rollercoaster."

"That's really insightful!" she said. Had anyone else uttered the words to Preston, he would've thought they were being condescending but Princess Yeona was so earnest that it was impossible to think she meant anything other than what she said.

Preston reflected on his words. It *was* exciting to go on a rollercoaster or to eat really spicy food or to watch a horror movie–even if it might also be scary. It was exciting to be here too, not knowing what was going to happen.

The Princess stroked Preston's leg. He didn't jump, too buzzed to be self-conscious.

"What are you thinking about?" she asked him. She tilted her head to the side in an absolutely adorable gesture.

"Just tipsy thoughts," he said.

Princess Yeona poured out the last of the soju into their cups, Preston once again surprised to see he needed a refill. She held her cup up to him, having him cheers her again. There was a finality about it.

"To tipsy thoughts," she said.

Preston laughed. "To tipsy thoughts."

They finished off the second small bottle of soju and Princess Yeona scooted the table away. It was time.

FOOLING AROUND

Princess Yeona looked at Preston. The cheeks of her round, sweet face were a rosy pink from the soju. She bit her lower lip and her eyes darted back and forth with his, trying to look as deep into him as he'd allowed. It was like being with a girl for the first time all over again, thought Preston. Even tipsy, he was nervous and didn't know where to look, or what to do. The Korean girl spread her latex-clad legs, inviting Preston between them. She leaned over and whispered hotly into his ear.

"I want to watch you suck me off," she said.

Despite that the latex strap-on was obviously not *actually* part of Princess Yeona, her whispered request was so genuine that Preston could've believed it was if he didn't know better. He slowly slipped off the bed and to his knees, taking the spot that the Princess had made for him. Looking at her from this angle was a mindfuck through and through–he saw the shiny black latex cock standing at unceasing attention and then for the first time took in the realistic looking latex testicles it had, which helped to create the illusion that somehow this protrusion was real. Still, Preston had no idea what to do, no idea what she wanted.

Reading his consternation, Princess Yeona said in a kind, soothing voice: "Just do what you'd like."

So Preston did. With Daddy Dong's pearl diving lessons still deeply ingrained in him, he gave the fake cock a big, lavish lick from base to head, feeling the bumps and curves of the realistic veining on his tongue. To his surprise, Princess Yeona groaned like she actually had a real cock that Preston was licking, the sound unbelievably convincing. It made him lick her again even more zealously.

She murmured something in seductive Korean and then said, "That feels *sooo* good, baby."

Preston continued lavishing the faux phallus with licks, which then turned into kisses and him taking the shiny latex head into his mouth. Princess Yeona gasped when he did that, even though he thought her eyes were closed, and he was too torn between being impressed with how she figured it out and too horny himself to worry about it. He brought "her" deeper into his mouth until he triggered his gag reflex without realizing it, causing Preston to choke and cough.

"Sorry," said Princess Yeona, her eyes fluttering open. "I know, I'm too big."

"It's okay," Preston heard himself say, unbelieving the words coming out of his mouth. He took the latex cock back in his mouth, bracing himself against his gag reflex this time so he could get her deeper inside. He still couldn't handle the size of her and Princess Yeona reached down to lovingly stroke Preston's hair.

"Lick my balls," she cooed in a husky, breathy voice.

Preston didn't know if she'd said that to spare him his gagging or if there was something more deeply pleasurable the entire exchange for her, but he obeyed nonetheless. He ducked his head down and ran his tongue across the mock balls, feeling the give of the latex and the wrinkle-texture under his lick. It was weirdly nice, all things considered, even if Preston had never had much interest in licking anyone's balls.

"Swirl your tongue around them," said Princess Yeona. Preston swirled his tongue and either the Princess could somehow tell or she assumed he would because she moaned a loud, lusty "Ohhhhhh FUCK" that almost made Preston think he'd done something to hurt her.

"You're good at this, baby," said Princess Yeona. Preston knew that couldn't possibly be true but he was too deep in their roleplay to think otherwise. Then the Princess said: "I want to fuck your pussy so bad."

Her words should've given Preston pause or made him shoot a startled glance, but they somehow made him swirl his tongue even faster around the dildo's fake balls, to which Princess Yeona responded with a long, drawn-out groan of bliss.

"I can't wait anymore," she said, eagerly. "I need it. I need *you*."

Princess Yeona sprung to life, reaching down to grasp Preston's head in her hands. She smiled at him and urged him off his knees as she stood as well, taking up a position behind him to then push him onto the bed, on his back She straddled him, the latex rubbing against his skin, and then craned her head down to plant heady little kisses down his chest and up his neck.

"Do you want me to fuck you?" she asked him overeagerly.

Preston knew what his answer would mean, but even so he found he was nodding at the bubbly, happy, sweet and cooing pretty Korean girl on top of him. Princess Yeona gave him a delighted smile back.

"Yes! I'm going to make you feel *soooooo* good, baby," she said.

Her hands were already on Preston's hips, trying to flip him over as she situated herself to one side. He let himself be turned over, not fighting the Princess as she adjusted his ass in the air and–somehow–found a hidden bottle of lube from somewhere on or in the bed to squirt down his ass crack.

"Show me that pussy," Princess Yeona said, lightly pulling Preston's cheeks apart with her hands and signaling him to do the same.

Delirious and drunk, Preston reached back and grabbed his ass cheeks. He pulled them apart. A second later he felt a wad of warm spit land right on his hole.

"Beg me to fuck you baby," she said, slapping her latex cock down Preston's ass.

"Fuck me," said Preston, feeling nothing like himself.

"Tell me you want my cock," said Princess Yeona.

"I want your cock," Preston said.

"Princess," said the Korean woman, pushing Preston to correct his speech.

"I want your cock, *Princess*," said Preston, annoyed and needy all at once.

Princess Yeona slapped her cock against Preston's asshole a few more times. "Don't worry, I'm going to give it to you baby," she said with a giddy little laugh.

Preston felt the Princess shift, moving the head of her strap-on towards his hole. The slick, fat head pushed up against him and Preston's breathing grew tight.

"Just relax," said Princess Yeona in a low, husky voice. She pushed the strap-on deeper and the copious lube between Preston's cheeks helped her sink into him. Along with her dildo, he felt the Princess's weight on him as she fought his puckered rim–she had done this before, many times, and she seemed to know how to let the lube and her own bodyweight do the work that her "dates" might not be able to do themselves.

For Preston, it was a seesaw between discomfort and acceptance. He would feel the latex cock pushing into him and, when he managed to take a breath, his muscles would relax, and Princess Yeona's pressing body weight would cause the phallus to sink deeper into him, inch by inch, with an intimate inevitability. Once she was deep enough in him, she let her body stretch across Preston's back, not caring how the spikes poking out from her bust dug into his back. She put her lips to the side of Preston's neck, planting a heavy, wet kiss.

"Your pussy feels so good," she whispered in his ear. Her tongue flicked the inner curves of his ear eagerly and she wiggled her hips against him. Her hands moved down to hold Preston by the waist, fingers pressing into his skin. "I'm gonna fill you allll the way up."

Princess Yeona's heady words helped Preston's hole relax and he soon was taking as much of her as he could, the Princess's shaft pushing hard against his prostate. His own cock was trying to grow between him and the luxurious bedspread, but was smothered into an achy half-erection that he tried to lift his hips to help relieve. The weight of Princess Yeona was too much though, and all he did was help her latex shaft sink into him another few slivers of an inch.

Her hands trailed up Preston's sides, stroking him. "You're such a good fit," she said to him joyously. She wiggled her hips some more. "My prince."

The Princess started to pump her hips. As she did, Preston felt the lubed-up strap-on ride his hole, bumping against his prostate. Preston grunted in a mix of pleasure and pain, and his cock hardened as much as it could, until Princess Yeona's pumping was causing Preston to rub against the silken bedspread. Despite his body pressing down on the bed, the soft pink comforter felt exquisite against him. He let out a shuddering sigh at the feel of it and his milked prostate.

"Oh god," he murmured, the soju still keeping his tongue loose.

"You like that?" offered Princess Yeona, gyrating her hips in a lazy circle, the tip of the strap-on pressed against Preston's prostate the entire time. He felt a heated little bead press itself up his shaft.

"Fuuuuuuck," he moaned. He was rocking his own hips against the bed now, forming a chain between the Princess's humping and the bedspread underneath him.

He jumped as Princess Yeona kissed his neck, hard, sinking her teeth against him. That was sure to leave a mark. Her hips sped up, pounding that sensitive spot inside Preston, her skintight latex squeaking along with the mattress springs. Her breath grew ragged and hot in Preston's ear.

"Yes, yes, yes," she chanted.

The way the Princess was moving made Preston think that she was somehow getting off on this too–mentally, perhaps, but maybe by rubbing herself against the base of the strap-on. The thought that the Korean mistress was building towards climax made Preston even more excited and he rocked his hips faster, cock rubbing hot against the silky sheets. Before he knew it, he was on the verge of cumming.

"I think I'm gonna cum," he said between breaths.

"I want you to, baby," said Princess Yeona. "Cum for me. Cum with my cock in your ass."

That was all it took to send Preston over the edge. He splattered himself against his belly and the sheets, surprised at how much had built up in his balls. And when he came, Princess Yeona seemed to as well–she dug her phallus deep in his ass and grabbed him tightly, moaning with ecstasy in his ear. They slowed their movements together and then Preston felt himself lying on a puddle of his cooling seed, the weight of Princess Yeona–spiked bustier and all–pushing into him.

Princess Yeona rested her head on Preston's back; he could feel her breathing. After a few strangely sweet moments of their embrace, the latex-clad woman lifted herself up, letting her cock slide out of Preston. He felt empty without it inside of him.

The Princess let out an accidental burp. "Woops," she said, laughing to herself. "Too much soju."

Preston carefully turned to the side on his back, pulling himself off the sticky semen. He was embarrassed to have made such a mess.

"I'm sorry," he said, not sure what to do with himself.

Princess Yeona beamed. "Don't be. This is what I wanted."

"You wanted me to cum all over your bed?" asked Preston, still feeling the effects of the Korean liquor.

"I wanted to pop your cherry," said Princess Yeona.

Preston blushed. Well, she certainly had done that.

"But now we're all messy," added the Princess.

"I know, I'm sorry," Preston said again.

"And I know–I heard you the first time," said the Princess, still as cheerful as ever. "Help me get out of this catsuit."

"The… the catsuit? Your catsuit? Why?" asked Preston.

Princess Yeona stuck her tongue out at him playfully. "So we can go in the soaking tubs together. I get sooooo sweaty under latex. You don't mind, do you?"

Preston didn't mind at all. He forced himself off the bed and clumsily helped unzip the skintight latex catsuit. He was amazed how much sweat there was underneath it, the Princess's body drenched and–once they had managed to peel off the entire outfit–shocked at how there were puddles of sweat in the hollows of the latex. He helped her unlace her boots, Princess Yeona stepped down to finally become shorter than Preston, and then they were naked together, like a bunch of young teenagers who had just been fooling around. Preston couldn't help himself–he looked down at her naked crotch, greedily looking at her fine brown-black hair.

Princess Yeona tilted Preston's head back up to look at her.

"Come on," she said. "Follow me to the bath."

He obediently followed behind her, staring madly at her cute little butt as they stepped back into the blue and pink neon lights of the hallway. He was hypnotized, knowing he would follow her wherever they went. They turned two corners and reached a wide doorway with an extra heavy hanging curtain that had a Japanese character on it. Preston could smell the bath salts and steamy water. As the Princess led him through the curtain, he saw there was a modest yet well-equipped spa waiting for them. It included a steamy hot bath that could fit six or seven, along with a sealed sauna room and several plastic stools set up next to a row of shower massagers.

"We have to rinse off before we use the bath," Princess Yeona said to Preston, pointing towards the plastic stools.

Taking her cue, Preston stepped over to one and turned on the water. It was pleasantly warm and Preston sprayed himself down, washing the cum off that had stuck to his chest and belly. But as washed off a coat of lather and began toweling himself off, he noticed that the Princess was just standing there, doing nothing. He looked at her curiously.

"What's wrong…?" he asked.

"I don't want to waste it," she whined.

Preston raised an eyebrow. "Waste what?" he asked.

The Korean mistress turned to one side and then the other, showing off her glistening, wet body. "My sweat," she said, as if it was the most obvious thing in the world. "I was thinking… would you like it?"

Preston huffed a laugh, not sure if he was even drunker than he thought. Did she really ask him if he wanted her sweat?

"Uh, sure," he said, still not really clear what he was agreeing to. "Why not."

Princess Yeona turned around, showing him her back and ass and the other side of her thighs and calves. There were fat droplets of sweat all done her lush skin. She pushed her hips back, presenting her ass to him. She didn't say it, but the message was clear–she wanted him to lick the sweat off her.

Preston came close and kneeled down on the tile floor. He didn't know where to start and so he started logically, licking from the back of the ankle of one leg, up her calve. It was sweat all right, salty and tinged with lotion and a lightly fruity perfume. He thought he could taste the soju they'd had and wondered if the Princess was sweating it out already. He drew his tongue up her calve, along the backside of her knee, and along the back of her thigh, getting close to her ass. He paused.

"Don't stop there," crooned Princess Yeona. "My butt is *really* sweaty."

Preston stared at the Korean woman's ass. It was small and tight and firm and he couldn't believe it, but he could imagine himself licking it, crack and all. Still it was like nothing he'd ever done in his life and with the effects of soju starting to wane, he wasn't sure he could go through with that level of perversion. Princess Yeona noticed his hesitation, but instead of calling him out on it, she encouraged him further.

"Put your tongue between my cheeks," she said quietly, conspiratorially, like two young lovers sharing a secret. "Go ahead. Do it do it do it."

Lolling out his tongue, Preston placed the tip of it at the bottom cleft of her cheeks. There was indeed plenty of sweat there, along with a very specific feminine musk that was also slightly soju-tinged. He started to lick up, letting the force of his tongue part Princess Yeona's cheeks.

Who AM I? wondered Preston.

The tip of his tongue dragged along the most intimate, sweatiest, muskiest part of the Princess and when he drew his tongue along the tiny little puckered rim of her asshole, she giggled.

"That feels nice," she cooed.

"Princess Yeona!" barked an angry, matronly voice. "What are you doing?"

Preston pulled his face out of the Princess's ass and looked towards the spa room's hanging curtain. Standing there was a Korean woman with a severe face and her hair pulled back into a low bun. She was older than Princess Yeona, but not far off from Preston's own age–mid-40s, he figured, maybe a smidge more–still maintaining that sheen of youth Asian women seemed to have. She was dressed in all black leather, the motorcycle jacket and straight pants and tall riding boots all boxy and angular on her small but imposing frame. She had a serious air about her that unnerved Preston.

Princess Yeona's face went pale. She quickly pulled herself away from Preston, covering up her breasts with one hand and her crotch with the other.

"Queen Haewon!"

Preston froze. Did she just say "Queen"?

ALL HAIL THE QUEEN

The stern-looking woman glared at Preston, then she looked back at Princess Yeona.

"You tramp! What in the world do you think you're doing taking strange boys into your bed?"

Princess Yeona shook her head fitfully. "It's not what you think!" she cried.

Somewhere in the back of Preston's mind, he was well aware that this was still the Silk Dungeon–and still part of his Omakase Package, but it all felt so real.

"I saw that boy's disgusting tongue on you," growled the woman–the Queen. "And I saw your sheets too! I'm going to have to have those burnt."

"*Eomeoni!* I can explain!" begged the Princess.

"Can you explain the empty bottles of soju as well?" asked Queen Haewon with an icy stare.

Princess Yeona grew quiet and the Queen turned her attention on Preston.

"You," she seethed. She marched over towards the plastic stools, not caring that her outdoor riding boots were on the clean tile, and she snatched Preston by the ear.

"Ow!" he whined as she went to drag him away.

"Don't *eomeoni*, he didn't do anything," said the Princess, offering only words as the Queen pulled Preston to his feet.

"I'm going to deal with *you* later," Queen Haewon hissed at the Princess. She tugged on Preston's ear, nails digging into his skin. "Come along, you disrespectful cur! I'm going to make you pay for violating the Princess!"

Preston stumbled down the hallway, naked and still dripping. The woman gripping his ear was a force of notice and despite being a head shorter than Preston and weighing at least fifty pounds less, she moved him with ease. They passed Princess Yeona's room and went down another forty feet before Queen Haewon dragged Preston through a black hanging curtain with silver lettering. The Queen flicked a switch on the wall, bringing up the room's brightness and blinding Preston in the process. He visored his eyes to try to make out his surroundings.

It looked like a royal sitting room, full of ornate furniture pieces with velvet upholstered in creamy jades and pristine pinks. There was a curved chaise and a vanity and several ottomans and a large, throne-like chair, all of it having a certain stuffy, almost frumpy quality to it. Queen Haewon kept an iron grip on Preston's ear as she brought him before the throne. It had a sculpted silver metal frame and pink cushioning that looked meticulously maintained. She sat down, her grip on Preston forcing him down to a kneeling position.

"What were you doing with the Princess?" the Queen demanded to know.

Something Princess Yeona had said to him before popped into his mind: *There are lots of ways to have fun. It just depends on your state of mind.*

This was a game, Preston realized. And the players were Yeona, the horny and mischievous princess, this woman Haewon, the controlling and wronged queen, and Preston–the unworthy interloper sneaking into the Princess's bedroom. He imagined how he would act in this situation–his role–and felt sure that a boy sneaking in to drink and flirt and fuck with the Princess would not give her up so easily.

"Nothing," said Preston, slipping into his role. "We were just talking."

"Lies!" hissed the Queen. "I saw the room! I saw the two of you! I can practically smell the little tramp all over you!"

"No, that… that was just me helping her get ready to bathe," stammered Preston.

The Queen's eyebrows arched severely. "Do you think I'm a fool? If you won't willingly tell me what you were doing, I'll make you tell me!"

Queen Haewon left Preston kneeling in front of the throne as she stormed off to her vanity. She grabbed a large hairbrush with a dark wood handle and cream-toned bristles and pushed an ottoman towards Preston, nearly barreling it into him. Grabbing him by the hair, she forced him over the jade velvet of the ottoman, belly-down.

"Last chance," warned Queen Haewon. "Tell me what you were doing with that miserable slut or else!"

But Preston couldn't rat Princess Yeona out–he wouldn't!–and so he kept his mouth shut, starting to tremble at the thought of being spanked with the hairbrush by this strict, mature woman who was probably only a year or two older than Preston himself.

"You filthy dog," she snapped, bringing the hairbrush down. She pulled no punches and the bristles landed hotly on Preston's bare ass. He yelped. The hairbrush fell again, but this time it was the wood side that hit Preston, the blow blunt and hard. He yelped again, feeling the cry deep in his diaphragm.

"I try so hard to teach her and guide her and she *betrays* me by bringing back classless riffraff into her bed," complained Queen Haewon, smacking Preston with the bristle side of the hairbrush several times, ignoring his growing cries. "I'm just getting started with you, dog. By the time I'm done, you won't be able to sit for a month!"

The Queen was serious about her threat–she brought the hairbrush down another dozen times, alternating cheeks and sides of the brush, building a burning, aching fire across Preston's ass. This was so much harsher than what he'd endured the night before at the hands of the visiting girls, their unpracticed, sloppy strikes feeling like they were a million years ago. Preston tried to get a breath in but every time he went to inhale, the hairbrush fell again, causing him to expel what little air he was able to get in a ragged, wet gasp.

His vision went blurry with tears, but he still saw when Queen Haewon held the hairbrush to his mouth.

"Hold this," she commanded. "And if you leave any teeth marks, I'll have every last one of your teeth pulled out!"

The logical part of Preston's mind knew that would never happen, but being deep in their roleplay, the threat felt very, very real. He held the handle of the hairbrush in his mouth, making sure to keep his teeth covered by the inward curl of his lips. It was hard to hold onto the hairbrush this way and it only got harder when Queen Haewon began to administer a spanking with her bare hand.

"You think you can come into my home and get my princess drunk and then roll around in her bed, do you?" the Queen asked, punctuating her questions with a steady beat of spanks. *Spank. Spank. Spank. Spank.* "You think you can drag my princess to the bathhouse and put your grubby hands and mouth all over her?" *Spank. Spank. Spank. Spank.* "Confess to what you were doing! Confess and tell me the princess's part in all this!"

Queen Haewon's spanking didn't waver for a second. Tears were rolling down Preston's face now and he was beginning to lose his grip on the hairbrush, wondering how much more he could take. His ass was on fire and his legs were shaking as the sound of the Queen's firm hand on his backside echoed throughout the room.

Spank! Spank! Spank! Spank!

The hairbrush fell out of Preston's mouth and clattered to the floor.

"How DARE you?" roared Queen Haewon.

If the spanking was intense before, now it was unbearable as the Queen brought her hand down faster and harder. Preston's tears turned to sobs and then into a full-body cry.

"I'm sorry," he blubbered.

"Sorry for what?" the Queen demanded to know.

"I'm s-sorry for drinking with the Princess," cried Preston.

"And what else?" *Spank! Spank! Spank!*

"And taking her to bed!"

"And what else?" *Spank! Spank!*

"And putting my tongue on her to lick up her sweat!"

"Disgusting!" *Spank!* "Filthy!" *Spank!* "Depraved!" *Spank!* "Whose idea was all this? Yours or the princess's?"

"The princess's," Preston cried out, realizing he'd just ratted on Princess Yeona.

Finally, after an eternity, the spanking stopped. Preston's ass felt like tenderized ground beef and the slightest brush of Queen Haewon's hand made him flinch.

"Well, now Princess Yeona is *really* going to pay for being such a little whore," said the Queen with gleeful malice. "But first, we're going to fix you so you don't go sneaking into any more beds!"

Leaving Preston splayed across the velvet ottoman, Queen Haewon stepped over to the vanity, where there was a large, heavy-looking leather handbag. She snapped it open and reached inside, pulling out a small metal device and a leather belt of sorts with what Preston immediately recognized as a butt plug made of stainless steel.

"Up!" ordered the Queen.

Preston shakily got to his feet, the Queen taking a set on the ottoman. His genitals were level with her mouth, although there was nothing sensual or seductive about her positioning. She grabbed cock and balls in one hand and shoved him into the small metal device, first through a thick base ring and then, after she had squeezed his balls through and tugged them down, pushed his cock into the device's smaller ringed shaft. It was already slick inside, making it easier for Preston's cock to slip in, but the Queen's grabbing and jostling of his cock made Preston start to grow erect.

Queen Haewon was prepared. At the first hint of his erection, she smacked his balls, sending Preston into a bowed-over groaning cry. She smacked him several more items, until the pain caused him to go flaccid again. The Queen hinged the device shut, its small hidden cylinder lock clicking shut. It was then that Preston could tell just how tight and small the device was, leaving him as nothing more than a covered nub with his balls hanging down exposed. Queen Haewon smacked his thigh.

"Turn around and bend over," she said. "Clearly that slut hole of yours needs to be locked away as well."

Feeling thoroughly chastised–literally and mentally–Preston shuffled around, bending at the waist. He heard the sound of straps and buckles behind him and then felt the cold kiss of the metal plug as she put its tapered tip to his asshole. It took was already slick and with the fucking he'd received from Princess Yeona, the plug slid into him with surprising ease. And, as it widened and Preston started to tense, Queen Haewon pushed it in firmly and decisively, making his legs shudder as it was fitted deep inside of him. She pushed on his chest to stand him up again and drew the straps of the belt attached to the plug around his waist, clicking their ends to the chastity belt. Then she took the last end–the one that went between his legs, and brought it around to his front. Preston saw that end of the belt was Y-shaped, and clipped into the chastity device and the other belt ends that were around buckled tight.

The result: Preston's cock was caged, his balls were exposed, his ass was plugged, and the entire setup was kept snug with buckled leather belt straps that made it impossible for him to push the plug out. There was something immensely controlling about being put into such a getup and simply by wearing it, the Queen seemed to take on even more power in Preston's mind.

She picked up the hairbrush and held it to Preston's mouth.

"Don't drop it this time," she warned.

Preston took it between his lips, remembering not to put his teeth on it. His eyes were downcast, his ass still itchy with pain. She closed her handbag and picked it up.

"Now come with me. It's time the princess was taught a lesson."

Preston followed Queen Haewon like a whipped dog, feeling the steel plug filling his ass. The push of it on his prostate made his cock swell, but the chastity cage was there to stop more than the slightest growth. He bulged against the ringed shaft of the cage with a dull ache. It was a miserable, dominating feeling and quite perversely the thought of it made Preston's cock try to grow even more.

They found Princess Yeona in the room from before. The cum-stained bedsheets had since been changed to a fresh set and the empty soju bottles and leftover cups had been cleaned up. Princess Yeona was sitting naked on the bed with her hands on her thighs, looking afraid.

"*Eomeoni...*" said the Princess, seeking mercy.

"Don't even try that on me," Queen Haewon spat out. "I know everything. Your little boyfriend here squealed."

Princess Yeona flashed Preston a betrayed look. He turned away, ashamed.

The Queen sat down on the other side of the bed. She patted her leather-clad lap. "Come here and take your punishment," she said.

With a despondent sigh, Princess Yeona stood up and went over to the Queen, folding herself over the older Korean woman's lap. Queen Haewon pointed to a spot on the floor beside them.

"You, dog. Kneel."

Preston got down on his knees. The Queen took the hairbrush from his mouth.

"I can't begin to tell you how disappointed I am," said Queen Haewon. "But I think you'll soon understand."

The spanking that the Queen gave Princess Yeona was even more vicious than the one Preston had received. The Princess held out for a few minutes, maintaining a silent, stoic air, but as the hairbrush painted her tight, trim behind a shade of deep pink, she started to lose her composure. She began to stomp her feet in pain, wriggling and writhing on Queen Haewon's lap, and before long the unceasing sound of the hairbrush's whapping was joined by Princess Yeona's desperate, pitiful cries. As Preston watched her ass jiggle with the spanking, he ached against his chastity cage. The sight of the young Korean woman being disciplined turned him on in a way he had never known before and he stared unblinking as Queen Haewon took out all her anger on the Princess's backside.

Queen Haewon looked at Preston. "You dirty dog," she said. "Even now, you're staring at the princess with that disgusting look in your eyes. Go ahead, dog. Get a sniff of her. Do it, now!"

Preston leaned forward and put his face to Princess Yeona's behind. He could feel the warmth radiating off of her. He inhaled, breathing in her musk and sweat and the distinct smell of her ass.

"Get in there, you mutt," said Queen Haewon. She took Preston by the back of the head and forced his face into Princess Yeona's ass crack, making his nose and mouth and lips rub along her sweat and heady scented skin.

"You're probably a mongrel of no nation, made up of all the discards from elsewhere. Is that why you defiled this Korean princess?" The Queen pushed Preston's face in deeper, his nose pushed into Princess Yeona's asshole for a brief moment. Then she shoved him away.

"I'm sorry *Eomeoni*," whined the Princess. "I'm sorry!'

Queen Haewon gave Princess Yeona a quick, mean spank to shut her up. "You don't even know what sorry is yet."

She pushed the Princess off of her, setting her face down on the bed with the hairbrush in front of the Princess's face. She picked up her handbag, setting it on the bed, and from it she pulled a belted device that looked an awful lot like the one she'd put on Preston, only this one had two stainless steel plugs protruding from its middle leather strap. Preston watched with morbid curiosity as Queen Haewon brusquely pushed the plugs into Princess Yeona's asshole and pussy, making the belt extra tight around her and locking it with two small little bronze padlocks.

"Get on your knees on the bed," the Queen said to the Princess. She turned to Preston. "You too. Face each other."

Preston climbed onto the bed, kneeling in front of Princess Yeona. Her face was streaked with tears, her makeup ruined and her face flushed from her hard crying. Her eyes glittered with tears and she turned her brows up at Preston, looking like she might start crying again any second. Queen Haewon pulled out a strappy, strange item from her bag, made of two O-shaped rings stacked together, with two straps extending from each side. She fastened it onto Princess Yeona first, and Preston came to understand what it was: a double-sided gag, meant to hold their mouths open and pressed together in an eternal kissing position.

When the gag was fastened tight, Preston was left to look Princess Yeona right in the eyes, his lips on hers. He wanted to put his tongue in her mouth, even with his betrayal of her, but fought back the urge. He throbbed in his cage and wondered if Princess Yeona aching with the plugs inside her, too. It was all enough to distract Preston as Queen Haewon readied the rest of what she had in store for the two of them, but when Preston heard the shrill jingle of thin chains, he looked frantically to see what the Queen was holding.

Nipple clamps, ones where the clamp seemed to slide and tighten when they were pulled. Queen Haewon attached one of the clamps first to the Princess and then to Preston. Even without being tightened, the bite of metal was nasty. Next, the Queen drew the ends of each pair of clamps behind Preston and the Princess, She threaded them through D-rings set along the top of the bed's twin stocks, adjusting the length of the chain so that it was just beginning to pull on Preston's nipples. He and Princess Yeona were stuck in their kneeling position then, where if either one were to lean back, they would pull the other one with them, causing the clamps to tug savagely on their nipples.

"Almost there," said Queen Haewon.

The Queen took two pairs of handcuffs from her heavy leather handbag and cuffed first Preston's and then the Princess's hands behind their backs. They were truly helpless now.

"Excellent," announced the Queen. "Now we're ready to begin."

Both Preston and the Princess looked nervously towards Queen Haewon. She reached into her bag and pulled out a small metal tube roughly the size and shape of a marker. In one quick motion she whipped it forward, extending out the nested inner tubes, forming a long, metal cane. Princess Yeona began to whimper in fear.

"What's wrong?" crooned Queen Haewon. "Aren't you two dirty sluts happy to be together again?"

Princess Yeona's stare darted to Preston, going so wide he could see the whites of her lidded eyes. He looked at her sadly, trying to apologize with his eyes.

"Remember, princess. I'm doing this for you," said the Queen. "To teach you a lesson."

Then the metal cane landed on Princess Yeona's ass.

She screamed into Preston's mouth and jerked forward, the butterfly clamps on her rosebud nipples tightening. She screamed again, though what Preston really noticed–shamefully–was how her leaning forward helped to ease the slack on his own clamps, giving him a moment of respite. Queen Haewon caned her again, prolonging Preston's relief as she cried into his mouth. Princess Yeona flailed madly on the bed, trying to do anything she could to ease the snakebite pain of the clamps. Queen Haewon raised the metal cane. It was Preston's turn.

She brought the thin metal down across both his ass cheeks. Even though it could've been harder, his raw ass made it sting so bad he too was sent careening forward, dooming his nipples to a savage bite by the clamps. He grunted into the Princess's mouth only to be canned again and then a third time, each one making him buck forward harder, pull his nipples tighter, and moan louder into the open gag he shared with the young Korean woman.

"Look at what you're making me do, *Yeona-ya*," griped the Queen. "This is all your fault."

Queen Haewon toyed with the pair for what felt like a long, long time, keeping them guessing who she would cane and how hard she would cane them. She wasn't satisfied until they were both sobbing again and their nipples were red and angry, their asses striped with cane marks. Finally the Queen relented. Taking off the clamps almost hurt as much as having them sharply tugged and Preston was afraid to look down, not ready for what he might see.

"I want to make something very clear," said Queen Haewon, tapping Preston's sore nipples with the cane. "If I ever catch you with my princess again, I will have you gelded—but not before I whip your testicles from here to kingdom come. Is that understood?"

Preston nodded, Princess Yeona's head bobbing up and down with him.

"And you," said the Queen, bringing the cane over to the Princess's nipples. She moaned. "You are going to remain in chastity for a long, long time, until you've earned my trust again. If I even see you make eyes at a boy, I'll have you wear a blindfold for a week. Do you hear me?"

Princess Yeona nodded and this time it was Preston who moved with her. The Queen collapsed her metal cane and dropped it back in her handbag. Slowly, she started to clean up—the nipple clamps, the hairbrush, their handcuffs. The last thing she did was to undo their joint gag, Preston and Princess Yeona sitting back on their heels. She had her eyes downcast, seemingly afraid to even look at Preston, and he looked across at her chest. Her nipples were red and swollen, with a flare of bright crimson all around them from the painful pulling of the clamps.

"You stay here and think about what you've done," Queen Haewon said to Princess Yeona. Then to Preston she said, "Come, dog. You don't deserve to be in my princess's sight."

Every step made Preston wince in pain as he limped after Queen Haewon. His ass hurt, his asshole hurt, his cock and balls ached, even the air brushing his nipples hurt. He followed the Queen back to her room with its jade and pink upholstered furniture and royal, stuffy designs. Queen Haewon set her handbag back down and let out a long, rolling sigh.

"Do you have any idea how difficult it is to raise a young woman in today's world?" she asked, rhetorically. "It requires constant vigilance and correction, always having to be the villain when that girl wants to spend all her time having fun and being irresponsible. It's utterly exhausting and almost leaves me with no energy to enjoy myself. But I do find my ways."

Queen Haewon reached down to her leather pants, finding a hidden zipper in the folds of the heavy material. It went all the way from front to back and when she unzipped it, her pussy was bared for Preston to see. There was a lush, thick strip of hair there, groomed into a classical, powerful style. The Queen sat down on the throne-like chair, moving her hips to its edge. She snapped her fingers at Preston.

He knew what was expected of him.

And so Preston got down on his knees once again for the woman who had plugged, belted, and beaten him, this time to worship her imperious, demanding pussy. Queen Haewon took her time cumming, allowing herself to relax as Preston desperately tried not to brush his abused nipples against the edge of the chair. With the woman's age came a deep knowledge of exactly how she liked to be pleasured and she was not shy about moving Preston's mouth and tongue to touch her precisely how she wanted, eventually settling into a lazy, leaned back position that ignored Preston as anything other than a trained tongue.

She came the same way she dressed and acted, with an unapologetic curtness spilled onto Preston's lips and ran down his chin. She did not offer him any words of praise or even a single smile afterwards. Instead she stood to zip up her leather pants again.

"You're dismissed, dog," she said. "Go clean yourself up at the baths and report to reception on the 8th floor. You have thirty minutes. Don't be late."

Queen Haewon stood by the doorway, waiting for Preston to leave her sight.

INTERVIEW WITH THE DOMINATRIX

The spa baths seemed far less exciting now that Preston was alone. He rinsed himself off with cool, lukewarm water, being careful with his ass and chest, and then he climbed into the steamy soaking tub, hissing out a wince as the hot water washed over his worse aches. He had no way to keep track of time and knew he couldn't linger for long.

He laughed. "That was insane," he said to himself, shaking his head. It was only then that his mind came back to Earth and the illusion of Queen and Princess and bad boyfriend faded, Preston impressed with how committed both Korean women were to their roles. But one thing was definitely true– the spanking and nipple torture Princess Yeona received was very much real.

Preston mulled over how that could be. Perhaps she enjoyed that kind of play too, as a kind of switch. It was an interesting thought.

After what Preston knew couldn't have been a little more than five minutes, he climbed out of the soaking tub. He rinsed off with more cool water and then patted himself dry. 8th floor reception. What could possibly be waiting for him there?

He went down the neon-lit hallway, looking out of the corner of his eye at Princess Yeona and Queen Haewon's rooms as he passed. Both were dark now, the Silk Dungeon mistresses now who knows where.

Preston called the elevator and rode up to the 8th floor. The doors opened yet again, and though Preston was expecting another hallway, he was instead met with a circular room with a round reception desk in the middle of it. He realized where he had seen it before–it was nearly identical to his own company's front reception desk. Sure, the little details were off–the wood grain was a little lighter and the desk height ever so slightly taller–but had he just glanced at it briefly, he would've thought he was on his way to work. Did the Silk Dungeon create this just for him? Did they have some storage room of furniture they used to stage these elaborate recreations?

Then another question popped into his head: Why had they set this up?

A smiling woman sat at the desk and for a moment Preston thought it was the female waiter. Only when he was closer did he realize it was someone else, someone he hadn't met before.

"Yes, hello?" she asked him with the stiff warmth of a receptionist.

"Uh, hi," said Preston. "I was told to come here…"

The woman tilted her head to the side. "You must be here for the job interview," she said.

"I guess so," said Preston.

"Are you…" The receptionist scanned a clipboard in front of her. "…Mr. Walton?"

"Yeah, that's me."

Extending out her hand, the woman indicated a row of three empty chairs against the wall. "Have a seat and we'll call you when we're ready for you."

"Um, okay. Great," said Preston, taking a seat. As he did, the plug in his ass bumped up against that sensitive button inside him and he shifted, trying to get more comfortable.

A job interview at a reception that looked just like his own. Another game, surely. But if his role in the last "game" was to be the lower class vagabond intruder, punished by the zealous and overprotective Queen, what Preston's role be in this game?

He waited. Five minutes passed, then ten. The receptionist typed at her computer and Preston started to wonder if they could've possibly forgotten about him. Such a thing was impossible but it nevertheless felt that way. Finally, after what seemed like a solid twenty minutes, the back door of reception opened.

A Japanese woman with rectangular glasses and long, wavy hair stepped out. Her face had a cutesy shape with a sharp jaw and little ski slope nose, her lips full and painted peachy-pink. She was in what Preston could only imagine was categorized as "fetish business wear"—a tailored black blazer with nothing but a see-through mesh tube top underneath, a too-short business skirt that left inches between its hem and the frilly tops of her flower embroidered lolita stockings, and a pair of ankle-strap pumps decorated with glittering rhinestones. The woman had a va-va-voom figure, all legs and hips and tits that made it hard for Preston to pull his eyes away.

"Mr. Walton?" she asked the room in a high-pitched voice, as if there was any way she could've possibly been looking for someone besides Preston.

He raised his hand.

"Hello, I'm Miss Sayaka. Please come with me," she said.

The office recreation ended at the reception back door and Preston followed the Japanese woman down a plain hallway. She walked like her striking, voluptuous figure was trying to burst out of her tight ensemble and Preston felt stiff in his new chastity cage, having to adjust himself several times and then race to catch up.

"We've had to reevaluate which positions you'd be a good fit for," Miss Sayaka said, not turning to address Preston directly. "According to your aptitude test results, we believe you'd be better as a part of our service team rather than the engineering management position you applied for."

Echoes of Lady Khan's comments rang through Preston's mind. The game was beginning to take shape.

"The service team?" asked Preston just as any curious applicant would.

"They're the ones who do the small jobs that keep this place running," explained Miss Sayaka. "We have several different positions open and today we'll be interviewing you for all of them to see which you're most suited to."

Miss Sayaka stopped in front of a closed, nondescript door. The plaque on it read: "Laundry".

As expected, inside was a laundry room, a simple, warm, bare bones one with a big, deep sink at one end, large canvas hampers lined up next to it, and a huge folding table in the center of the room. Laid on the table were three pairs of colorful, garish panties.

"Our company has us working very, very hard and we have to save time where we can. The staff's underwear is collected together, in this bin here.," said Miss Sayaka, pointing towards a woven laundry basket on one side of the table. "This isn't all of it, of course, but for today's interview we've gathered underwear from three of our members. Please take a look."

Preston stepped around to the table and saw that the three panties laid out on the table each had a small name sign next to each: "M. Yeona", "M. Sayaka", "M. Fei". Not only was it interesting to see Princess Yeona referred to differently here, but he wondered who "M. Fei" was as well.

"Your job is to sort the underwear from the basket," said Miss Sayaka.

Looking over the panties, Preston tried to decipher a pattern. The first pair, Princess Yeona's, was a pink with white trim lace V-string. The second, Miss Sayaka's, was black satin. The last one, belonging to the mysterious "M. Fei", was a simple red cotton bikini cut.

"It's the fabric," said Preston, like an overeager student answering in class.

"First are lace, second are satin, third will always be cotton…"

Miss Sayaka brought her peachy-pink lips together in a disappointed kissy face. "You think the members of our company only wear one fabric of underwear each?"

Clearly Preston was wrong. His shoulders sagged.

"Mr. Walton, we're not expecting you to crack codes here," said Miss Sayaka with a sigh. "Our service team members just have to learn to do what they're told, so please listen."

The chiding needled Preston and he couldn't help but look across the panties again, desperately seeking some actual code or pattern he could break. Miss Sayaka continued.

"It's simple, really. We each have our own unique smell. All you need to do is match smell for smell."

Preston looked up at the va-va-voom Japanese woman with the wavy hair. She adjusted her glasses. Did she really just tell him to sniff the panties?

"Yes, go ahead," she said, as if reading his mind. "Please take a smell of each underwear."

So Preston did. He held up each pair of panties, one at a time, trying to figure out the signature smell they had. It was a hell of a lot harder than he thought it'd be. Princess Yeona's seemed light and sweet and floral, Miss Sayaka's also light, but more grassy, maybe earthy, and the smell for "M. Fei" flummoxed Preston, like he was smelling a hint of some herb he couldn't remember the name of. He smelled them all again, trying to commit the smells to sense memory.

"Are you ready?" asked Miss Sayaka. "There are twenty pairs of underwear in the basket. You will have five minutes to sort them."

Twenty pairs. Five minutes. Preston did the math–that was four pairs a minute, one pair every fifteen seconds. He could feel his anxiety rising, his heart speeding up like he was at the start of a big test. He took one more quick sniff of each of the panties on the table, only thinking once he'd started how much it looked like desperation.

"Begin," said Miss Sayaka.

It was a mess. Preston picked up each pair of panties from the basket, giving the crotch and ass of it a deep sniff. There were thongs and g-strings and briefs and styles he didn't know the names of, made of lace and satin and cotton and nylon and silk, ranging from subtle creams to eye-searing neon yellows. He was instantly lost and tried to let some deep, inner instinct guide him as he inhaled the faded female fragrances on the unwashed underwear. When he was halfway through the basket, he looked to see how he'd distributed the panties so far–the piles were uneven, favoring Miss Sayaka and "M. Fei", and Preston felt whatever mental algorithm ticking away in his head adjust, knowing that by the law of large numbers there were likely to be a roughly even number of panties for each woman.

Five minutes passed in a flash.

"Time's up," Miss Sayaka said.

He looked at her with trepidation, not wanting to jinx himself by admitting how wrong he thought he was. She stepped over, short skirt and lolita stockings brushing against him as she went to correct his work. He watched as she moved a pair from the Princess Yeona pile to the Miss Sayaka pile. Then a pair from the "M. Fei" pile to the Miss Sayaka pile as well. In fact, *every* pair of panties was being moved to the Miss Sayaka pile and by the time she was done correcting Preston's work, he realized that every single pair had belonged to the Japanese mistress.

"I don't think Laundry is the right fit for you," she said, putting a polite glaze on her words.

The criticism stung Preston, as did the thought that Miss Sayaka had just watched him sniff her panties for five minutes while sorting them all wrong. He blushed a bit, feeling eminently incompetent.

Miss Sayaka righted her posture and gestured towards the door. "Come on, Mr. Walton. Let's move on to the other service team positions."

He followed sullenly behind her as they went further down the hallway, her stockings swishing. They stopped at a room with a sign that said, "Break Room".

Half-expecting to see some kind of clever, sadistic take on what a "break" room might be, Preston was surprised to see that it consisted of an ordinary and well-worn leather couch and a small kitchenette with a meager strip of counter space next to it. On the countertop was a coffee pot and a rack with cups and saucers. Miss Sayaka stepped over to pour herself a big cup of coffee, the light steam rising from it suggesting the coffee wasn't piping hot. She opened up the cabinets above the cupboard and pulled out a pack of Seven Stars cigarettes and something that looked like a cross between an ashtray and a dental mold.

"We've been meaning to get a new table in here for ages, but we can't decide on which one to get," said Miss Sayaka, her back still to Preston. "In the meantime, we have members of our service team filling in. Go and get on your hands and knees in front of the couch please. Facing me."

Preston stepped over to where he thought a table would go and got down on all fours. He faced Miss Sayaka, his lower position allowing him a slight peek up her skirt. He couldn't be sure, but he thought he spied a pair of ruffled red panties, the color of Valentine's Day. She turned, bringing the ashtray-dental-mold device with her.

"Open your mouth," she told him.

When he did, in went the device, the mold settling between his teeth. The mistress motioned with her hand for him to close his mouth so that he was now holding the ashtray in front of his face. It was clean, but much like the leather couch it had been used often, old ash stains still marring the thick black resin. Miss Sayaka retrieved her coffee, along with a lace trim doily that she rested on Preston's lower back, right above his sore bottom. He felt the warmth of her cup and saucer as she rested it there and then heard her take out a cigarette and light it. A cloud of light, sweet, milky smoke wafted towards him.

"It's very important to take breaks throughout the day," Miss Sayaka said, leaning back onto the couch.

She lifted her feet to put them on Preston's upper back, the rhinestones on her ankle-strap pumps sinking sharply into his skin. Along with the smoke, he caught a whiff of her too, the mix of lotion and light sweat reminiscent of the panties he'd been sniffing. The intricate embroidery of her stockings chafed his skin slightly as she adjusted herself, growing roughly as the mistress bent over to take a sip of her coffee or to ash her cigarette in the ashtray in front of Preston's face.

"We encourage our teams to take at least an hour of break time throughout the day, including lunch. All in all, you would be expected to provide table service for approximately three to four hours a day. It's stationary work, as you can tell, so no heavy thinking is required. You should do fine with it."

The heat of the coffee was beginning to get to Preston. He took slow, deep breaths to steady himself, trying to think of anything else but the slowly growing heat. Miss Sayaka suddenly took her shoes off Preston's back, sitting up.

"I'll be right back," she said, slotting her still-lit cigarette into the side of the ashtray. Its cherried tip burned inches away from Preston's face, the smoke curling up directly into his eyes and up his nose.

Miss Sayaka clacked her way out of the room and down the hall.

Preston waited for her, watching anxiously as the cigarette continued to burn. The smoke grew thick, its sweet and milky scent becoming cloying, but Preston had no choice but to breathe through his nose, filling his lungs with the increasingly noxious scent. His body started to tremble. He'd stood on his feet for hours at a time, so he thought all fours would've been just as easy or even easier, but he'd never been forced to balance a cup of coffee on his back before. He knew it couldn't be *that* warm, but the longer it stayed on him the more it felt like the doily underneath was being ironed into his skin. He wiggled his toes and clawed his fingers into the floor.

Where was Miss Sayaka?

The cigarette had a quarter inch of ash now and Preston's eyes were watering from the thick blue smoke. He exhaled out his nose, hoping to blow the smoke away, but all that made him do was have to take an even bigger breath in. He fought back a cough. Just then the door opened, Miss Sayaka returning.

"Sorry, I had to use the ladies' room," she said, sounding like she had just raced back down the hall. "If nothing on the service team works out for you by the way, we could also use more tongues on the janitorial staff." She explained no more than that, letting Preston's imagination fill in the rest.

She plopped down on the couch again and put her shoes back up on Preston's back, ignoring her cigarette.

"I really should give up smoking," she lamented. "One of these days. The smoke, it just gets on *everything*. In your hair, on your clothes, on your furniture…"

The more the mistress talked about cigarettes and smoke, the more Preston felt like he could taste it in his nose and mouth. His near-cough got worse and the thought of him nearly coughing made him want to cough even more. He was holding his body tightly now and it caused the doily and cup-and-saucer set to slide down his lower back, towards his raw ass. The smoke grew thicker and the rhinestones of Miss Sayaka's pumps dug in deeper. Bullets of sweat beaded his forehead now and arms began to feel like jelly.

"I've been thinking about having someone from the service team provide table service for me at home," said Miss Sayaka, in one of those "big ideas that'll never happen" musing tones. "Might be good to have a side table when I'm getting my makeup ready in the morning, or when I've got a man over and I want to have some toys laid out to play with…"

The cup-and-saucer scooted further down Preston's lower back as the image of the voluptuous Japanese woman in bed made Preston's cock stir in its cage, the man shifting to relieve it. Miss Sayaka lifted her shoe off Preston.

"Or even to practice my penmanship," added Miss Sayaka. "My *kanji* are getting so ugly."

With her nail, she began to draw a character on Preston's back and the sharp cut of her strokes was the last straw—Preston lost his concentration, coughing from the smoke, which in turn sent the hot cup-and-saucer onto his ass. He bucked wildly, spilling the coffee and throwing the cigarette and ashes to the ground. Miss Sayaka let out a long, frustrated sigh.

"You can't do this right, either?" she asked. "Please tell me you're not going to waste my *entire* day."

In a petulant huff, Miss Sayaka brusquely pulled out the ashtray-gag, letting it tumble to the floor. She ground out the lit cigarette under her shoe. There was a mess on the Break Room floor, all thanks to Preston.

"I can clean this up," he offered meekly.

"Forget it," said Miss Sayaka, still very much annoyed. "One of the janitors will lick it up. They're good at their jobs."

The insinuation was, of course, that Preston was not. Miss Sayaka stepped towards the door, impatiently motioning for him to follow. Two interviews—and two failures—down. How many more were left?

"Let's try something simpler," mumbled Miss Sayaka as she clacked deeper down the hallway. "Even you should be able to master this."

BREATHTAKING

The next room they stopped in front of had a sign that read, "Reading Room". Inside it was like a mini library, with bookshelves and racks of glossy magazines all around, a good number of them in non-English, Asiatic languages. Preston breathed a sigh of relief. Books. He could deal with books. Even if he had to organize books in other languages, he'd figure out something. Maybe he'd have to hold a book for Miss Sayaka to read from or even read to her while she closed her eyes. Yes, it was all very doable, Preston felt sure of that.

He held back a smile.

"This is our reading room," explained Miss Sayaka, trying to push through her annoyance. "It's where we come when we need a mental break, where we refresh our minds, spark our curiosity, and learn something new to talk to each other about. This is where you're needed."

Preston looked around, not seeing what Miss Sayaka was pointing to until he looked down. There was a padded pink leather box of sorts on the ground with a circular cut out on top. Looking closer, Preston saw that one side of the box had been removed and that the interior was foam molded to fit the back of someone's head.

"Down… there?" asked Preston. "In that, uh…"

"In the reading stool, yes," said Miss Sayaka, like it was the most obvious thing in the world. "Go ahead."

She tapped her shoe on the floor impatiently, waiting for Preston to comply. He got down on his back and wiggled himself into the "reading stool", his head just fitting against the molded foam, his face pressed against the padded leather box's circular opening. Miss Sayaka crouched down, sliding two panels on the open side of the box together to press lightly against Preston's neck, preventing him from pulling his head out of the box.

The mistress began to look for something to read.

"There are rules in the reading room," said Miss Sayaka, scanning a rack of Japanese magazines for something in particular. "It's meant to be quiet in here, peaceful. So all you have to do is help facilitate a quiet and peaceful atmosphere by not making a fuss yourself. There really isn't much more to it than that."

Miss Sayaka found the magazine she was looking for. It was a large format beauty magazine, with bubbly Japanese writing across its cover. She put the magazine under her arm and then hiked up her short skirt, revealing the ruffled panties underneath. As Preston had thought, they were Valentine's Day red and made of a shiny, silky satin, cut into a high-waisted V in front and nothing but a beaded thong string in back.

She sat down, her behind descending right on top of Preston's trapped face. Her cheeks were warm on his skin, the weight of her pushing the back of his head against the molded foam base of the seat's inside. Miss Sayaka didn't hold back her weight in the slightest and Preston's face soon felt heavy and flattened; he took in a strained breath, inhaling the bouquet of her sex. Even with the pressure mounting in his face, Preston's cock surged in its ringed cage, the harsh metal denying him anything more than a meager half-erection. Miss Sayaka settled down further so that her red satin panties formed a seal over Preston's mouth, his nose pushed hard against her barely-covered taint. She flipped through her magazine.

Preston's heart beat heavily, unable to see anything other than the mistress's high, smooth ass cheeks pressed against his eyes. He breathed in again. His lungs had to work twice as hard for this breath and drew in half as much air, his inhalation fighting the thick, musky satin that covered his mouth. Miss Sayaka murmured to herself and flipped the page of her magazine, mumbling something in Japanese about whatever beauty article she was reading.

The thin breath Preston had taken was soon used up by Preston's strained, nervous body. His lungs burned. He tried to get more fresh air, but his labored breathing had made Miss Sayaka's red satin panties damp and when he tried to breathe in again, all he got was wet satin and the tickle of the mistress's pubic hairs through her panties. His heart beat faster as panic started to set in.

Preston tried to pull his face away from Miss Sayaka's crotch but the reading stool held him firmly in place. He sucked on the damp satin again and as he did, Miss Sayaka wiggled herself down onto his open mouth. He could feel her pussy lips against him and he heard her murmur again, letting out a small, little sigh. There was the distant sound of a magazine page flipping and a wave of dizziness washed over Preston.

The panic grew. Preston pushed his nose along the mistress's taint, seeking oxygen, but all he got was the intimate, musky scent of her backside. Miss Sayaka said something in whiny, irritated Japanese and then shifted her hips up, offering Preston a small sliver of space. Her cheeks still resting on Preston's face, he felt her tense and then there was the slightest hissing sound, followed by a pungent waft of foul air. Miss Sayaka sat back down and Preston was forced to inhale her expelled gas. He gagged and tried to recoil, having no recourse but to fill his lungs with her fart.

More page flipping. More muttered, annoyed Japanese. Preston clenched his fists determined to endure for as long as he could. His vision tunneled and a bright, white hot fear prickled throughout his body. His feet danced frantically. His body bucked. No, he couldn't do it. He needed air, he HAD to breathe. He inhaled as hard as he could, determined to draw breath in through the damp panties, but there was no air to get, just the feel of the mistress's pussy and the scent of her sex. Preston bucked again, trying to push her off. He kicked his feet and slapped the box, reaching up towards Miss Sayaka to try to push her off his face.

The mistress grumbled out another long string of exasperated Japanese. But she did not move.

What the fuck? thought Preston. *Why isn't she moving? She knows I need to, knows I can't stay like this knoooooooooooooooooo*

ooooooooooooooooooooooo

ooooooooooooooooooowwwsss.....

Everything became slow and distorted. Preston's thoughts drifted away, like in a dream. He imagined himself showing up to the last day of classes in college, completely naked and unprepared for the gauntlet of finals that awaited him. It was like Princeton but not, all the students replaced by faceless Japanese women in schoolgirl uniforms. They were studiously hard at work on their tests while Preston looked for his seat. He couldn't find it. He was forced instead to go up to the lecturer–also Japanese and female, but dressed like Miss Sayaka–and take off his cock and balls to trade them in for a tiny wooden seat. The Not-Sayaka lecturer took his genitals and put them in a small wooden box that she locked with a tiny padlock. Then he sat in the too-small seat and realized the entire test was in indecipherable Japanese.

"–ton. Mr. Walton!"

Preston's eyes fluttered open. Looking down at him through his hazy vision was Miss Sayaka, her brows furrowed and her lips pursed.

"Sleeping during the interview? Do you even want to work here?" she asked him angrily.

He had passed out, Preston realized, smothered into unconsciousness by Miss Sayaka's ass. He took a deep breath, inhaling her bouquet along with precious fresh oxygen. Miss Sayaka freed his head from the reading stool. She was beyond disappointed and put her magazine back while mumbling something in nasty Japanese under her breath.

"Mr. Walton. There is just one more position we have here but I have to say I am beginning to think you are not going to work out as part of our service team. I beg you to take this next interview seriously. Do you understand?"

She left Preston to extract himself from the box, although she did offer an arm as he woozily stood up, bracing the nearest bookshelf until his head cleared. He took several more breaths while his world came back into focus.

"Are you ready?" asked Miss Sayaka.

Preston nodded, though he couldn't have felt less ready for anything in the world.

They stopped at one more door, this one labeled "Package Room". Preston imagined some kind twisted mailroom, where he had to lick envelopes until his tongue was raw or where he had to haul boxes back and forth until his muscles gave out or some other impossible, humiliating task meant to make him feel inferior and insufficient.

Miss Sayaka opened the door. It didn't look anything like a mailroom. A bedroom, maybe, but not a mailroom nor a Package Room. There was a hip-height cushioned table that was like a bed but not, looking more like a comfier version of an examination table upholstered in dark purple pleather. A double-doored dark wood cabinet was across from it, covered in cherry blossom designs, and to the cabinet's side were two black lacquer chairs flanking a round table. A plush gray shag rug covered almost every inch of the floor.

Preston was completely confused. How in the world was *this* a "Package Room"?

Miss Sayaka stepped over to the cabinet and opened the double doors. A light inside stuttered to life. Instead of liquor bottles though, the warm, cozy light illuminated two rows of standing dildos of all shapes, sizes, and colors.

Ah, Preston thought. *A "Package" Room.*

He was suddenly reminded of the steel plug filling his ass. His eyes anxiously flicked over the rows of dildos, trying not to focus on the largest, most intimidating ones lest Miss Sayaka's attention be drawn to them. The Japanese mistress looked them over carefully, lost in thought. She drew her fingers across them, tips grazing the faux phalluses and making each wobble ever so slightly as she touched them. Many of them looked terrifyingly lifelike to Preston, as if they'd been plucked right off some poor man's crotch.

Preston thought about the semi-dream he had after he'd passed out from Miss Sayaka sitting on his face: Trading in his cock and balls to get a seat to take a goddamn final exam of all things. How fucking lame.

Miss Sayaka picked a cock. It was fat and pink and covered in obscene, thick ribbing. She handed it to Preston to hold. It was uncomfortably heavy. Then she opened a drawer at the base of the cabinet and took out a strap-on harness.

Preston held in a sigh.

She took the dildo from him and slotted it through the strap-on harness's ring, making sure it was nice and snug. But she didn't put on the harness. Instead, Miss Sayaka handed it back to Preston, leaving him to hold it as she unclasped her short skirt and unzipped it, letting it fall down to her ankles.

She doesn't want to mess up her skirt, thought Preston.

Her ruffled Valentine's Day red satin panties followed next, revealing a completely shaven pussy, the lips petaled and pink.

She wants to feel the dildo against her, thought Preston, becoming less confident by the moment. What was going on?

Miss Sayaka kicked away her skirt and panties. Her eyes flickered up at Preston.

"What are you waiting for?" she asked. "Put it on."

"This?" asked Preston, holding up the strap-on harness. "Why?"

"Because you can't fuck me when you're in chastity, can you?" Miss Sayaka asked back, her tone on edge, like Preston had asked some irritatingly obvious question.

The meaning of the room was becoming clearer. Its "package" wasn't for Preston–it was for Miss Sayaka, and any other mistress who might use it. He fumbled with the harness, never having put one on before, and as he worked to fit it to his body so it sat above his caged cock, Miss Sayaka stepped panty-less over to the dark purple table. She sat down on the edge of the table, unbuttoning and shedding her tailored blazer so that she only had on the sheer, see-through mesh tube top underneath that hugged her heavy, bouncy breasts. She opened her stockinged legs, teasing the sight of her shaved, pink pussy, ready to be fucked.

And it was Preston who was supposed to fuck her. Sort of, anyway. He adjusted the harness as well as he could, the lewd pink dildo dwarfing his own chastised member. It was surreal to look down and see another dick jutting out from his crotch, especially one longer and girthier than his own.

"I'm waiting," the Japanese mistress said.

Of all the ways Preston thought he might have to submit at the Silk Dungeon, never in million years did he think he'd be told to actually *fuck* one of the Dungeon's mistresses. The idea of a man fucking a woman seemed inherently *un*-submissive to Preston, if by nothing else than by virtue of how masculine and controlling and dominating he'd always viewed sex. Man puts cock in woman's pussy–what could be more dominating than that?

But nothing felt dominating about this, and it wasn't just the fact that Preston was to use a dildo to fuck Miss Sayaka. She was the clear recipient of pleasure here, the one to *be pleased*. Even if Preston's cock hadn't been in its chastity device, he would've felt like he was there to perform for the mistress and not the other way around.

He stepped over to Miss Sayaka, fake pink cock jiggling madly back and forth. The mistress was already dewy with anticipation. She said something in Japanese to Preston. It sounded like a command and he was pretty sure of its meaning:

Fuck me.

Preston's body count was not just pitiful, it had mostly occurred during clumsy, unsure nights, leaving him with no sense of whether he was good at sex or not. He had assumed the worst, which only discouraged him from trying, creating a negative feedback loop that has been a jarring contrast to his rising career success. According to Lady Khan though, even that success was bullshit built on getting lucky. And if that was bullshit… maybe, just maybe, Preston's insecurity and lack of confidence was bullshit too.

Preston moved towards Miss Sayaka with renewed swagger. As he came close, she leaned back and lifted up her stockinged legs, hooking them on Preston's shoulders, the rhinestone-studded backs of her tall heels scraping his skin. He didn't care. He drew the head of the dildo down her lips to push it into her, the mistress's position making it easy for the pink phallus to disappear into her wetness. She moaned encouragingly and Preston wished he could feel her for himself.

He squeezed his hips, the shaft dipping into Miss Sayaka until Preston could feel her warmth right up against his own crotch. His caged cock bumped the cushioned table as a stark reminder that Preston wasn't *really* penetrating the mistress. Like he needed one. The kiss of confining metal did spark a fire in his belly though—the leggy, bombshell Japanese mistress had delighted in grinding Preston down and now he had to fuck her too, without feeling anything?

Preston thrust the dildo into her with a twinge of anger. She gasped.

She wants to get fucked? thought Preston, that fire inside growing quickly. *I'll fuck her alright.*

He grabbed her stockinged legs and pulled out until the head of the dildo was stretching her lips. Then he pumped the cock deep in Miss Sayaka's pussy so hard her breasts bounced wildly in their mesh prison. She gave him a sultry look, her lips gently parted. This was exactly what she wanted.

Preston worked up to a grunting, thrusting hate-fucking rhythm. His grip on her legs was so tight that the embroidery underneath chafed his fingertips and he let his body slap against her so hard that the sound of their bodies smacking together filled the room. He grimaced and glared at her and the mistress threw her head back into the tumbling pile of her wavy hair, letting out a throaty moan.

This isn't enough, thought Preston, his hair wet with sweat, his chest heaving. He pulled the strap-on out of Miss Sayaka to her shocked gasp and then roughly turned her over on her stomach so that she was bent over the side of the cushioned table so that Preston could take her from behind. She arched her back and he slid the dildo back into her. Then he grabbed her hips and started fucking her like a wild, rutting animal, each thrust sending a shockwave through the woman and making her slide up and down the dark purple pleather, ass wobbling, hands barely able to hold on. A jolt of inspiration coursed through Preston and he slapped Miss Sayaka's ass, and he was rewarded for it with a long, lusty sigh from the mistress.

Preston didn't care that he'd never been this person before. He was this person now, transformed at Miss Sayaka's behest. He dug his fingers into her hips and pounded her pussy as hard as he could. He could ignore his caged cock and not being able to feel her, though the one thing he couldn't fully ignore was the plug in his ass which seemed to fuck him as he fucked her. Preston used its ceaseless thumping to feed that fire inside of him, taking out the anger of being treated like a plugged, caged fuck-toy on Miss Sayaka's pretty pink pussy.

The mistress slipped a hand down between her legs to play with herself. It didn't take long before she was crying out in desperate Japanese through a shuddering orgasm. Only when she quieted and Preston slowed down his pumping did he notice just how thick the smell of sex was in the "Package" Room. His heart felt like it was going to explode. He pulled the dildo out of her, his own cock so swollen in its chastity that he could feel his pulse down there too. A sheepish look fell over him as Miss Sayaka turned over to face him once more. She was beet red from the neck up.

As she let out a happy sigh, relief flooded through Preston.

"Yes, I think you'll do nicely here in the Package Room," she decided. She pointed towards her flushed, wet pussy. "Help me clean up."

Preston got down on his knees between Miss Sayaka's stockinged legs and licked her gently, cleaning away her wetness and, in a very different sort of inspiration, planting soft kisses up and down her lips and along the insides of her thighs. His rage was evaporating and in its place was an odd kind of devotion. Preston didn't exactly know what to make of it, other than it felt like they had actually fucked and now he was providing tender aftercare.

When Miss Sayaka was ready, she nudged him away and got dressed. She asked Preston for the strap-on harness and deposited it in a bin hidden beneath the double-doored cabinet. She cupped his full, aching balls.

"Our service team stays chaste 24/7," she murmured. "It helps them focus, we've found."

Miss Sayaka patted his balls patronizingly.

"Come along, let's get your paperwork filled out."

Somehow, the mistress managed to maintain her composure after the hard fucking she'd just taken, showing no signs of it other than that her swaying walk was ever so slightly muted. Preston, on the other hand, felt like he was walking bow-legged to accommodate his stifled cock and plugged ass, sure that he looked like some awkward circus monkey following behind its handler. They returned to reception.

"Get Mr. Walton processed for the service team. He'll be working in the Package Room," Miss Sayaka said to the receptionist.

The receptionist nodded dutifully and went straight to frenzied typing.

Miss Sayaka retreated to the office and, before she went through the back door, she added:

"And remove his garments. He should enjoy a little freedom before he's put into full lockdown."

Then she was gone. The receptionist opened a drawer and pulled out a small ring of keys, coming around to unbuckle and unlock Preston's cage, plug, and belt. She tweezed the entire ensemble in one hand and dropped it in a bin on the other side of reception that looked like the one in the Package Room. Preston was free again, his ass gaping and his cock throbbing excitedly.

"I believe you have a lunch appointment now, Mr. Walton," the receptionist informed him. "Top floor. Dining room. I believe you're familiar with it."

Preston was. His pointing cock led the way to the elevator, where he hit the button for the top floor, feeling pretty damn good about himself, though he didn't quite know why.

COME TO YOUR SENSES

The elevator opened onto the private dining room with its 360-degree view of San Francisco. The horseshoe of tables from last night was gone and there was only one table left, set up on the dining room's raised stage. Seated there was Mistress Midori in a stylish V-neck, belted green jumpsuit. Preston crossed the empty dining room to join her. Spread across the table was a sumptuous dim sum feast with almost two dozen little plates laid out for them, along with pots of tea, carafes of coffee, and bottles of sparkling mineral water.

Preston sat down, his buttocks still tender from Queen Haewon's hairbrush spanking.

"You're looking… virile," teased Mistress Midori.

Self-conscious of his newly-freed erection, Preston shifted the table clothing so that it covered him up. Mistress Midori laughed.

"That's not what I meant," she said, though she didn't elaborate. She turned the table–revealing that its top rotated like a giant Lazy Susan, perfect for their dim sum feast–and served herself some pork buns and shrimp rolls.

When she was settled, Preston turned the table back, serving himself a similar assortment, along with sesame balls and egg tarts. The food was pleasantly warm and incredibly fresh, and Preston suspected that some of the city's dim sum chefs had to work here at the Silk Dungeon on the side. The two of them ate in silence for a few minutes, Preston's gaze wandering to the wraparound windows. Low cloud cover created a layer of fog that weaved through the downtown buildings, making the streets below hazy and mysterious. Even though they weren't that high up, the fog nevertheless made it seem like they were nestled in some secluded spot in the sky, away from the day-to-day dealings of the world.

Yes, Preston really *did* feel good about himself, he realized. It wasn't just being let out of the chastity device either. He felt rejuvenated, somehow. Revived. He almost wanted to say he felt…

…strong.

But how in the world could he feel strong from a day of being teased, taunted, humiliated, and denied?

"Something on your mind?" asked Mistress Midori.

"Earlier you said the word 'jealous' was interesting," Preston said. "Can you tell me more?"

Mistress Midori paused her eating. "It's not an interesting word to you?" she asked back. Seeing the stymied look on Preston's face, she laughed softly and added: "People will do all kinds of things for their jealousy, just like they would for someone they're in love with. But jealousy is the worst kind of lover. It feeds off your weakest parts and twists you into something not to heal and strengthen those parts, but to hide them, covering them over with nice clothing, fancy cars, gorgeous partners, and other shiny badges of status until you aren't even you anymore. What's most insidious about jealousy though is how long it takes to change you, the process so slow that you don't even notice it happening. Then, one day, you look in the mirror and realize you're wearing a mask, with nothing beneath."

Preston listened, speechless. *It feeds off your weakest parts.*

"And for me that means...?" ventured Preston.

"Exactly," said Miss Midori.

"So you're not going to tell me."

"I think I just did." Mistress Midori started eating again. "Don't worry, you'll have time to think about it."

Preston picked at the food, not particularly hungry anymore. He came here for adventure. They threw him into the unknown. He was told he wasn't as sharp–special–as he thought. He had pussy shoved in his face, constantly. He… envied. That was right. He envied the men who could attract these women, just like how he bristled at Miss Midori's mention of Miss Grace's boyfriend yesterday. He had to admit, he was jealous. But as important as that revelation felt, there were still missing pieces to the puzzle.

Mistress Midori noticed that Preston had stopped eating. "Are you done?" she asked him.

"I guess so," said Preston, trying not to act too petulant.

"If you have to use the bathroom or anything, this would be the time," she told him, pointing towards the restrooms next to the elevator.

Preston heeded her advice and went to take care of himself. He almost didn't recognize himself in the mirror. Usually, the face staring back at Preston was Preston the Engineer, Preston the Successful, Preston the

Nerdy. But this version was something else. He kept thinking about how he'd turned Miss Sayaka over on her stomach in a fit of lust-rage, how he'd slapped her ass almost as hard as he could. It wasn't as if Preston had suddenly discovered some dominant alpha male side–more like he'd assumed a role, where Miss Sayaka was the hot girl with the outrageous body and Preston was the guy who got to fuck her silly.

Back in the dining room, the single table topped with dim sum had been wheeled to the back of the stage. Mistress Midori sat at its edge, smoothing out her green jumpsuit; she had pulled a chair next to her, several items piled on top of it.

"Come up here," she said.

Anxiously, Preston ascended the stage and as he did, Mistress Midori picked up a blindfold-like item off the chair. It had some sort of glossy, dark lenses on it, almost like thin, tinted ski goggles. She handed it to Preston.

"Put it on?" he asked her.

"Put it on," she said.

The blindfold-thing was very snug and tight and even though Preston could see there were only lenses to it and no actual blindfold, he still couldn't see anything with it over his eyes. He was then very aware of how close he was to the stage's edge and inched backwards.

"Stay where you are," said the mistress. "Don't move and you're fine."

Mistress Midori wasn't done with him. To a soundtrack of jingling metal, the mistress clapped a tall, cold metal collar around his neck before she put what felt like tight irons around his wrists and ankles, seemingly having to secure them with some kind of turn-screw that took a minute for each cuff. Chains joined these cuffs–heavy chains in fact, and in Preston's eyes he started to imagine himself like an old-timey prisoner, the kind that wear "manacles" and not handcuffs and who are forced to carry the weight of their bindings along with the misery of not being able to freely move their arms and legs. The mistress guided his bound hands up and clipped something snapping to his collar and wrists, preventing Preston from being able to lower his hands past chest-level. Another clip-lead of some kind followed, a taut length of chain that ran from his ankles to his wrists. That made it so Preston now couldn't move his hands from side to side either and the metal bindings were starting to feel very claustrophobic.

But he didn't know that was only the start.

"This is going to be the most disorienting part," she warned him. "If you begin to feel dizzy or like you might fall, let me know immediately."

Preston nodded, nervous. He felt something placed on his head–a headphone band with huge cups that covered his ears–and as it settled against his skull, he felt the pressure differential of the headphones' noise cancellation. The headphones crackled to life.

"Can you hear me?"

"Yes," Preston said, his voice sounding very far away.

"We're almost done," said Mistress Midori. "Here, hold this." She put something into his hands and then he felt it flick to life. Through his dark lenses it looked like a flashlight, illuminating a small spotlight around him, helping him maintain his balance. "It's UV light. It cancels out the polarization of your lenses. You can have it, for now."

Preston understood why she had given it to him when she pressed a large foam block between his teeth, forcing his mouth wide open and gagging him. She fastened it behind his head and then guided him so that his back was to the rest of the dining room and disappeared, leaving him standing there bound, deaf, and near-sightless. Mistress Midori left him like that for minutes that felt so much longer and while Preston had little sense of his surroundings, he did feel a mild vibration, like a piece of furniture being wheeled through the room. He breathed in through his nose, anxious that he couldn't get enough air.

Mistress Midori hazily reappeared, her hand reaching for the flashlight. "I'm taking this," she said, her voice filtering through the noise-cancelling headphones. The flashlight clicked off and, left in total darkness, Preston felt the mistress take it away.

"We're going to play a trust game," she spoke into his ears. "Take a step backwards."

It took Preston everything he had to step backwards in his heavy chains. His chest was tight and he wished he had his hands free to catch himself should he fall, testing his bindings and finding no give to them.

"Step backwards," Mistress Midori said again.

Preston took another step backwards, the edge of the stage looming in his mind.

"Another step," said Mistress Midori.

The next step Preston took was tiny and he very slowly let his foot fall, waiting to see if there was ground underneath. He had to be close to the edge now. The thought of slipping off without his senses, without being able to do anything to break his fall made his stomach churn. When

Mistress Midori's hand touched his chest, Preston flinched and nearly jumped backwards.

"I'm going to push you," the mistress said in his ears.

Preston shook his head no, the gag keeping him from protesting.

"Do you trust me?" she asked.

Her question gave him pause. He supposed he did, given the Omakase Package he'd signed up for. He'd put himself in her and the Silk Dungeon's hands and–so far–nothing had happened to make him feel like his trust had been violated.

He slowly nodded his head.

"On three then," said Mistress Midori in his ears. "Three. Two. One."

She did exactly what she said she was going to–she pushed him right off stage. There were several long, slow moments of freefall and Preston's pulse-racing panic became weightless, powerless peace. He landed on something soft and cushiony, like foam padding all around that seemed almost like it was perfectly shaped to his body, his hips and elbows and feet settling in as Preston caught his breath.

The UV flashlight turned on above him and he saw a vague silhouette of Mistress Midori standing at the edge of the stage. She shined it down on Preston and he lifted his head to see that she had pushed him into what looked like a large rectangular box with, as he guessed, soft cushioning. The flashlight clicked off again.

Wait... thought Preston. *Why am I in this thing?*

More movement, too much to be Mistress Midori alone. He felt the vibration of large furniture joints being snapped free and then refitted and felt the contouring foam around him squeeze his body; at some point two or maybe three sets of hands nudged him this way and that, perfecting the fit of Prestin on what was beginning to feel less like a cushioned rectangular box and more like a coffin.

When the bulging cushioned "lid" of this box-coffin was placed on top of Preston, he really started to panic.

It was clipped on in several sections, first from his knees down, making it so he couldn't even move his feet, then from mid-torso down to his thighs, the cushioned panel shaped to down his cock and balls while leaving room for the swell of thighs and then his neck and chest. There were vibrations as someone clambered on top of the box-coffin, though the construction was so sturdy he couldn't feel their weight on him, only their slight vibrations. The UV light clicked on and Mistress Midori was sitting cross-legged over the panel covering Preston's chest. He saw an eerily illuminated grin.

"This next part is tricky," she said. "Don't panic."

Telling someone not to panic was like telling them not to think of an elephant. She reached down and undid Preston's gag, tossing it aside. Then she held the interior of a mask over his head. The UV light wasn't strong enough to let Preston make out the details, but he did see one thing–the mask was being lowered on his face, large enough to cover every inch not packed in tight by the foam tubing.

What followed was a moment of true panic as the mask's shallow nostril holes and tongue depressor went into his orifices. He bucked, pointlessly, his attempted thrashing only revealing just how little he could move in what was now beginning to seem like a sarcophagus. The mask clicked into place, its "eyes" made of the same lens material of Preston's blindfold. It didn't matter though because a moment later, Mistress Midori turned off the UV flashlight.

"Try breathing through your nose," she said to him through his headphones.

Preston did so, grateful that he could get big lungfuls of breath in–although the cushioned padding kept him from breathing too deep.

"Now try your mouth," she said. He noticed after she spoke she left whatever push-to-speak microphone she was using on, a faint crackle of static audible to Preston.

He breathed in and there was an odd sound over his headphones, like a feminine moan. Then he breathed out and there was another odd, feminine sound, that of a relaxed sigh. He breathed in and out again, hearing the same sounds in his headphones, mixed with Mistress Midori's laughter.

"Perfect," she said, a smile in her voice.

Forgetting about the tongue depressor, Preston tried to speak. He couldn't hear anything but when Mistress Midori's voice crackled back to life, he knew she'd been laughing at the garish sounds he must've made in his attempt.

"I'm going to give you a little time to think about our conversation," she said, drumming her fingertips on Preston's mask so that he could feel the vibrations up and down his cheeks. "In the meantime though we need this room, so you'll be stored away somewhere safe. Enjoy."

Then there was only silence and the feeling of Preston being rolled away in his padded sarcophagus prison.

MALE ORDER

Preston had no idea where he'd been "stored" but he did know it took several minutes of rolling and an elevator trip to get him there. Then he was left in the still, empty expanse of his own mind, his only way to interact with the world around him through the bizarre, humiliating feminine sounds he could make that he himself couldn't even hear.

He descended into his thoughts.

I asked the mistress to explain more about jealousy and me and she said 'Exactly', he thought. *How was that supposed to be an answer?*

Jealousy. Wanting. Success. These women of the Silk Dungeon, these hot, confident women that Preston kept wanting.

Do you like Asian pussy?

He was barely able to answer Miss Ying when she asked him that, but of *course* he did. He was wild for it, crazy about it, had wanted it ever since he became interested in girls like that. And even with all that wanting, he had only slept with three women in 30-odd years of post-puberty.

And as Preston knew, none of those partnerships were anything to write home about sexually, either. One was a starfish type who just laid there, as if waiting for everything to be over, and the other two were mousey, quiet types who wanted Preston to take charge. But even when he tried to, they stayed so damn demure, acting shy and reserved and all "yes-I-want-it-but-I-won't-say-I-do'. Preston hated it and he hated how they seemed to want the vanilla, dumb horny male stereotype to constantly be hounding them for sex. It made Preston pull away, until they had sex less and less and then, eventually not at all.

Yes, I think you'll do nicely here in the Package Room.

As wild and cathartic as it felt to fuck Miss Sayaka with the strap-on, it still didn't feel right to Preston either. But playing that role sure was nice. It was the role he thought all those jocks and douchebag bros had played in high school and college, the ones who hooked up with the girls Preston *really* wanted, the cool Asian chicks, the hot ones with fiery attitudes and quick tongues. He remembered in college how he would hate-imagine some of his crushes being with their boyfriends, and the way he pounded Miss Sayaka from behind and slapped her ass so hard it left a handprint mark was exactly how Preston thought those people fucked in college.

He had definitely been jealous of that, even if…

Even if I didn't want to be those guys and do the things they did, thought Preston, an epiphany rising up in the sensory-deprived corners of his mind. *I didn't want to dominate them. I wanted them to dominate me.*

Memories crashed down on Preston: long nights at Princeton's Firestone Library, his first SWE job, his first promotion, the acquisitions, the first time his bank account made him laugh with joy, the company paid trips across the world, the quiet of meeting rooms when he spoke, the girls interested in him for his authority at work, the girls interested in him for his money, the girls interested in him for how he could network for them. Power. That's what those women saw in him. Fueled by spite and rejection, Preston had amassed power to *make* women want him.

But the funny thing was, he never wanted the ones who wanted him.

His third base hookup. The last time he'd been with a woman. It was a one-night stand out at some dive with a girl he met at the bar. She was sarcastic and pushy and all edges, not to mention hot as fuck in her torn denim jeans and Ramones tee and motorcycle jacket. Preston had felt outmatched by her wit but she didn't seem to mind, maybe even liked that a little. They wound up at her place. It was a dumpy little apartment in a sketchy part of the city. After they made out like their plane was going down, she rode his face while sucking Preston off, his first and only 69 ever. After they were both sweaty and satisfied and he was getting ready to go home, he promised he'd text her the next day.

In the morning though, all Preston could think about was that ramshackle apartment and how far away from his own success it was. He never texted and, when she eventually messaged him, he ignored it. She didn't message again.

He still thought about her from time to time.

Lying in his padded sarcophagus, Preston laughed, not caring what kind of obscene female sound it made. This seemed like a fitting position for him: a supposed leader like him all packaged up and placed in an ornate casing, left alone with his faux greatness for all of eternity.

What am I doing with my life? he wondered. *Is this all there is? Meetings and product launches and bonuses? Maybe more importantly… what* could *my life be?*

He let out a long breath, comforted by the fact that the sensual, relaxed sigh the mask over his face would make would at least somewhat capture his state of mind, albeit a twisted mirror version of it. He was not relaxed nor satisfied, but he did feel the weight of a heavy sigh inside that needed to be released.

His mind drifted on, meandering through thoughtspace, coming back to his regrets and wants and missed opportunities over and over. There was no escaping them and Preston thought if there was a hell, it might be existing this way forever, never able to get away from all the things you wished you'd done differently.

Something touched the mask over Preston's face. It was pulled off him, the tongue depressor and nostril tubes slipping free. Preston took a deep, greedy breath through his mouth. The headphones came next and Preston worked his jaw to pop his ears. He heard the panels sealing him into his sarcophagus clip free and felt cool air on his sweaty, warm body. Soft hands unclipped the chains connecting his collar with his wrist cuffs and then with his ankle cuffs, dropping the chains on the hard floor. The turn-screws for the manacles were undone one at a time, each removed piece of bondage making Preston feel lighter and lighter.

The last thing to be removed was his goggle-like blindfold. His collar had been left on. His eyes struggled to adjust to the bright light.

"Hello there," said a voice Preston didn't know.

His vision cleared.

Standing over him was a woman with skin so pale and snowy white it seemed to glow, and if Preston believed in angels, he would've thought she was one. Her hair was a waterfall of shimmery black ink that went all the way to her hips and her gentle curves were encased in an elegant red silk qipao dress with a slit that went all the way up one leg, teasing what was underneath. The dress's Mandarin collar was wrapped tightly around the woman's graceful swan neck and twin sets of pankou knots studded the bust in an upside V, giving her an air of sophistication.

The woman clasped her hands together and smiled to herself. "We're going to have so much fun," she said.

Her voice, like her clothing, was refined and distant. She unfolded a sheet of paper. The bright lights overhead let Preston scan the text from the other side and although he couldn't read the print he could see that the sheet looked like an order invoice. As the woman reviewed the invoice, she looked down at Preston, eyeing him from head to toe.

"You look two inches shorter and a few pounds heavier than what's here, but everything else looks in order," she said. Without a hint of hesitation, she reached between Preston's legs, feeling up his cock. She gave him a pearly white smile. "Yes, everything's here alright. Come with me, *baipizhu*."

Preston climbed out of his padded prison. It was astounding just how well-fitted it was to his frame, leaving him to wonder how the Silk Dungeon had made it so perfect. When could've they taken such exact measurements?

The sleepsack from last night, he thought, impressed. He followed behind the woman in the red silk qipao dress.

"I am Madam Fei," the woman said. "You will not speak to me unless instructed to do so and when you do, you will refer to me as Madam. I've not acquired you for your thoughts."

Acquired you. Another roleplay, this time a reversal on the gauche mail-order bride from Asia trope, only it was Preston who had been ordered. Madam Fei led him through a narrow passageway covered in red damask wallpaper that opened up into a circular, domed bedroom that had a Chinese watercolor mural on the ceiling. The chamber had a circular bed in its center covered in a traditional Chinese comforter with an embroidered image of a dragon and phoenix, along with characters Preston had seen before. A paneled folding screen veiled the space behind the head of the bed.

"Lie down," she ordered him.

Preston stretched out on the bed, feeling the embroidered silk on his back. Madam Fei nudged Preston's arms and legs into an X and then, from under the bed, she pulled up red lengths of rope that had already prepared slipknots at the ends of them. The rope was soft on Preston's wrists and ankles and the mistress used a single rope at the foot of the round bed to tighten all the knots at once. After she tightened the knots, she pulled out an ornate, enamel pill box and took out a blue, diamond-shaped pill. Viagra. Madam Fei put the pill between Preston's lips.

"Swallow, *baipizhu*," she said, giving him a heavy bead of her spit to swallow with.

Then she disappeared behind the folding screen.

Preston pushed his head back, just able to see the screen over the mound of silk pillows at the head of the bed. Flickering candlelight illuminated the mistress's figure. He watched her long fingers work at her dress, peeling the silk from her graceful, willowy body. The viagra was kicking in already and

Preston's cock became hard as steel, jutting up unabashedly from between his legs. A smell filled the room. It was light jasmine and rose, with an undertone of spicy cinnamon and creamy vanilla. Wisps of incense curled up towards the domed ceiling from behind the paneled screen. Madam Fei spoke in sultry Mandarin, Preston unsure if she was murmuring to herself or speaking to him even though he had no idea what she was saying.

His cock grew even more engorged, feeling harder and thicker than it ever had in his life. It was almost painfully hard, the head swollen and the veins along his shaft pulsing with each heartbeat. He tested the red rope slipknots and found that as he pulled one side, the opposite side tightened–left hand pulling right foot, left foot pulling right hand. Preston felt like a trussed up piece of meat, a *thing* to be enjoyed by Madam Fei.

Excitement flooded through him.

The mistress stepped out from behind the folding screen. She was completely naked, her eyes dancing with delight as she looked at Preston's throbbing cock. Preston stared at her body–she had teardrop breasts that bounced light as she walked, slender hips with a pert peach backside, and a wild mane of dark feathery hair covering her crotch.

"*Baizhu weiyi shanchang de jiushi zuo'ai*," she said in Mandarin, smirking to herself. She nodded at Preston. "Right?"

Not knowing if that was permission enough to speak, Preston nodded back and Madam Fei laughed. She climbed onto the bed and straddled Preston's chest, sitting so that her pubic hair and warm lips were pressed down on him. The mistress gave him a joyful look, like he was the gift she'd wanted all year long and finally gotten. She traced her fingers along his upper chest and shoulders.

"*Zhu xiang chi lingshi ma?*" she asked, lowering one breast towards Preston's mouth. He kissed the nipple and, when she didn't pull away, he ran his tongue around it in circles, the nipple getting hard between his lips. Madam Fei brought the other nipple to Preston and he did the same, enjoying the feel of her downy skin on his tongue. "*Zuo de hao, baipizhu.*"

Then the mistress sat up straight and touched her hard nipples, sighing as she squeezed them between her fingertips. She inched backwards until Preston's cock was against her ass. She lifted herself up, hovering over him, and then gave him a stern stare.

"I know *baipizhu* like you have no control, but if you spill inside me without permission, there will be punishment," she warned.

Madam Fei sat down on Preston's cock.

She was fabulously tight around him, squeezing herself so that she gripped his shaft in a way Preston had never, ever experienced before. He grunted as he fought back a delirious wave of pleasure. Madam Fei started to rise and fall on him, sighing and playing with her nipples as she did.

"*Wo de shenti xiang yao,*" moaned Madam Fei, her indecipherable Mandarin lilting and melodic. She threw her head back, her waterfall of hair tickling Preston's balls each time she sat down all the way on his cock, making him suck in an inhalation through his teeth that filled his lungs with the floral, spicy-sweet incense smell.

Preston knew he was already dangerously close to cumming. He stared up at the Chinese mural across the ceiling to try to distract himself from Madam Fei's graceful, lithe figure. The intoxicating sensation of her pussy around him was as wonderful as it was maddening, and Preston had to keep stopping his body from tensing up to drive towards release. As he studied the mural, he saw there was more to it than just wispy trees and meandering streams. The trunks above were undeniably phallic, with thick bases and their branches pruned to look like swollen mushroom heads, and the streams were painted into sultry deltas, the land where the streams split covered in light, dark brush. Preston turned his head away, his brain back to thinking about sex.

"What's wrong, *baipizhu*?" taunted Madam Fei. "Can't you control yourself?"

He writhed and sighed, hands clenching and releasing.

The mistress sat down hard on Preston and gyrated her hips slowly, drawing Preston's embedded cockhead all along her tight, warm, wet inner walls. He grunted, angrily, the pleasure too intense. Madam Fei wagged her finger at him condescendingly.

"No cumming," she said. "Don't do it."

But even as she repeated her warning, her gyrations became more lusty and wanting. Preston could feel the bounce of her backside on his thighs and the rub of her wet lips on his crotch and all the while Madam Fei kept her eyes trained on Preston's, catching his gaze every time his head lolled towards her as he whipped it back and forth, trying to distract himself.

"Don't do it, *baipizhu*," Madam Fei said again.

Preston clutched the embroidered silk comforter in his hands. His toes curled. His breath came in quick little frantic puffs. Madam Fei's gyrations turned into a rolling, humping, rocking motion of her hips, running her tight pussy up and down his shaft as she moved forward and back, forward and back. Her breasts jiggled delicately.

"*Yu nuxing xiang bi, nanxing chuyu ruoshi,*" said Madam Fei. "*Ni tai ruole. Wo hen qiang. Ni jaing qufu yu wo de yizhi.* Isn't that right, *baipizhu?*"

With her mocking, rhetorical question, the mistress pushed herself down hard on Preston's shaft and grinded herself against him. He could hold on no longer. He burst inside of her, Madam Fei continuing to grind on him as she milked out every last drop of seed from Preston's heavy balls. He let out a roaring groan of euphoria and defeat.

Madam Fei's grinding came to a stop. She tut-tutted in disappointment and carefully lifted herself off of Preston, being mindful of his cum inside her. For a stomach-churning moment, Preston thought she was going to straddle his face and spill it onto him, but he was relieved when she disappeared behind the folding screen again to clean herself up.

"You shouldn't have done that," said Madam Fei from behind the screen. But the elation in her voice betrayed the meaning of her words. "Now I have to punish you."

Still naked, Madam Fei stepped back into view with a velvet drawstring pouch that she set on the bedroom's lacquered dark wood floor. Going in a circle around the bed, she undid the slipknots.

"Go stand in front of the bag," she commanded. "You will perform *san gui jiu kou zhi li.* The three kowtows and nine prostrations."

Preston clambered up off the bed, the joy of his orgasm fading as he took up his position in front of the velvet drawstring bag. He looked at Madam Fei and she snapped her fingers at him.

"You will keep your eyes down and follow my instructions to learn the positions you will take for this ritual. It is used to show remorse, submission, and the belief that the person seeking forgiveness–you, *baipizhu*–are at the mercy of the one they are bowing to. Me."

Madam Fei talked Preston through the positions. First, the kowtow, which required Preston to get down on his knees, head bowed and his hands placed palms-down on the floor, lowering himself until his forehead also touched the floor. The next position was the prostration. This was more comprehensive and it required Presto not just to get down on his knees but to also touch his hands, forehead, elbows, knees, and even toes to the ground, so that his body was fully extended in a straight line.

"Your kowtows are ugly and your prostrations are a disgrace," spat Madam Fei. "But we do not have time to turn pigs into people. It will have to do. You will perform three kotows and then you will perform nine prostrations. After each prostration, I will show you forgiveness by walking across your body. Do you understand?"

"Yes, Madam," said Preston, his voice dry.

He waited for her signal to begin. But before she gave it to him, she picked up the velvet drawstring bag. She turned it over in front of Preston and from it spilled uncooked grains of rice. His eyes widened and Madam Fei let a silence open between them, daring him to speak up. Preston did not. Madam Fei put the empty drawstring bag on the bed and stood ahead of Preston so that his bowing head would wind up right before her bare feet.

"Begin, *baipizhu*."

Preston had never felt anything like the biting pain of the uncooked rice grains. He winched through the first kotow, not a single part of his shins, palms, or forehead spared from pain. He held the position for a beat and then returned to a kneeling position to perform it again, each time getting more and more rice grains stuck against his skin, all while Madam Fei watched wordlessly. By the third kowtow, Preston was fighting hard to keep from making noise but he kept quiet, fearing Madam Fei would make him start again if she wasn't satisfied.

Then came the nine prostrations. While his body was spread across more surface area—making each uncooked grain hurt less than it would've against a smaller portion of his body—Madam Fei's steps across his back and ass and thighs made sure that every part of Preston experienced its own private hellish pain. He grew dizzy with the agony, unable to believe how slow it was taking to kneel, extend out, be walked upon, and bring himself back to a kneeling position. Preston thought the tortuous punishment would never end, almost unable to believe it when he finished the last prostration and Madam Fei finally spoke.

"Stay on your knees," she told him.

The mistress kicked aside the rice grains to one side so she wouldn't accidentally step on them. She moved in close to Preston, pushing her still wet pussy in his face.

"Worship me," she demanded, the grains of rice still digging savagely into Preston's legs.

Calling on the morning's training with Daddy Dong, Preston got to work, able to taste his cum mixed in with the mistress's tangy, strong sex. The only silver lining was that it didn't take long for Mistress Fei to climax, the willowy Chinese mistress shoving his face against her wild bush as she moaned through waves of bliss. When she was done, Preston was allowed to stand.

"We have to get those rice grains off of you," she said, picking up the velvet bag.

Holding it by its purple woven drawstring, she whipped the bag against Preston until she'd knocked away every last uncooked bit of rice. She threw the bag on the floor.

"Clean up your mess, *baipizhu*."

Madam Fei sat on the bed and watched Preston collect the two hundred odd grains of rice off the wood floor. It took him forever to tweeze up every last grain and when he was done he offered the drawstring pouch bag to the mistress. She took it and opened it back up.

"I didn't tell you to give it to me." She spilled out all the grains on the floor once more. "Do it again."

After another painstakingly slow clean up, Preston stayed kneeling with the bag in his hands, his eyes downcast as he waited for instructions from the mistress.

"That's the thing about people like you, *baipizhu*, you always have to tell them everything twice." She took the bag from Preston and placed it back behind the folding screen, taking her time to also put her qipao back on.

"It's time to get you ready," she said, once she had adjusted the silk dress. "For your trial."

THE TRIAL OF PRESTON WALTON

Preston wanted nothing more than to ask Madam Fei what his "trial" meant, but she'd already set the rules on speaking, already smothered his chances of understanding. He knew there couldn't be that much more to his Omakase Package. Was this the finale? And if so, what would the final verdict be?

The mistress led Preston by the ring hanging from the front of his collar, pulling him along to another Chinese-themed room, this one smaller and more severe, packed with red wood furniture and black leather padded surfaces. From a cabinet in the wall, Madam Fei pulled out a plastic-wrapped square clothing pouch. She threw it at Preston's feet.

"Put that on, *baipizhu*."

Inside was a black and white striped prison uniform, the weight and feel of the fabric cheap and disposable. The ill-fitting shirt scratched Preston's skin as he pulled it on and he saw that there were numbers across the chest: 121911. He pulled the pants on. They were also poorly fitting, too tight in the thighs, too loose in the lower legs, and the crotch was missing, exposing the bottoms of his ass cheeks and his genitals.

Madam Fei snapped her fingers, signaling Preston to follow. They went to the very end of the narrow passage with the red damask wallpaper, to a door that looked like it belonged to a supply closet. The cinderblock-lined space beyond didn't feel like part of the Silk Dungeon, reminding Preston of electrical rooms and emergency stairwells as they made their way to a service elevator with a pull door. The mistress rang for the elevator and a shrill bell went off twice. They waited.

When the elevator trundled to their floor, Madam Fei pulled the door open and motioned Preston inside. She pulled the door shut and hit the bottommost button, B2. The elevator shuddered its way down the shaft. Its slow descent gave Preston time to think.

His trial. That meant he was to be judged. The prison uniform rubbed against his skin as he tried to take a deep breath in. He had no idea what he would be judged on and somehow Preston already felt guilty.

The elevator came to a halting stop at the B2 level. Madam Fei brought him to a nondescript door, much like the one upstairs.

"After you," she said.

What awaited Preston on the other side of the door was a funhouse version of the private dining room on the top floor of the Dungeon. It was clearly the same footprint as the space upstairs but instead of a stage, this room had a hulking, black steel judge's bench with macabre flourishes right out of a gothic nightmare. There was a witness stand to one side and in front of it, some fifteen feet away, were peeling, beat-up wooden stocks raised three or four feet off the ground. To the side of the stocks, set just a little bit behind so that whoever was inside couldn't see, was a juror's box with eight seats. All but one was occupied.

In place of the 360-view windows upstairs were instead huge blown up prints–of Preston from the past 24 hours. Him being led around like a dog, him in the sleepsack, him licking the fake silicone pussy, him drinking soju with Princess Yeona, him sniffing panties, him tied.to Madam Fei's bed. Everywhere he looked he saw evidence of his submission at the Silk Dungeon.

Preston looked over the familiar faces in the juror's box, all dressed as when Preston had first laid eyes on them. Miss Ying and Miss Grace, in their fitted, dark navy officer's uniforms, with caps and epaulets; Lady Khan in her chic business outfit on her powerful frame; Daddy Dong in her crimson bodysuit, proudly wearing her piercings; Princess Yeona, changed back into eye-popping, spike-covered black latex that hid whatever marks she had from Queen Haewon's discipline; Queen Haewon with her angular, boxy leather jacket and pants; Miss Sayaka in her blazer and mesh tube top combo with the short skirt and embroidered stockings.

Before Madam Fei joined them, she pushed Preston over to the stocks, swinging the wood open and putting Preston's head and wrists against the half-circle cutouts. She let the top half of the stocks slam shut, startling him. She latched it shut and kicked his feet over to two latching ankles cuffs that kept Preston's legs spread slightly more than shoulder width. Then she joined the other mistresses in the jury box. Preston looked at the judge's bench, having to crane his neck slightly, where Mistress Midori sat in a black fishnet bodystocking that conformed to her voluptuous curves. To one side was a set of silver scales, to the other a single coin.

"Now that we're all here, let the Trial of Preston Walton commence," announced Mistress Midori.

At some hidden signal, all nine women gathered brought their hands together at the same time in a single loud clap that echoed throughout the shadowy space.

"Preston," Mistress Midori said. "You are here to be evaluated by the mistresses of the Silk Dungeon. Depending on what we decide, we will either end your Omakase Package with a celebratory reward or a suitable punishment. As we hear from the mistresses, you are not to speak. You will have a chance to speak after they have said their piece."

Bent over in the stocks, Preston felt a slight breeze between his spread open legs. Mistress Midori turned to the women in the juror's box.

"Each one of you has been part of these proceedings before but I will review your duty for our defendant's benefit. One by one, I will call you up to the witness stand, at which point you will give your judgment of this man here. After your judgment, you will step up to my bench and place the coin you have with your name on it on the scales."

Mistress Midori indicated the silver scales. One side's plate was adorned with tiny little cherubs, the other with impish devils. The implication was clear.

"Let us begin with you, Miss Ying," said Mistress Midori.

The modelesque tall mistress with the harsh features stood up and sauntered over to the witness stand. She looked to Mistress Midori.

"The question for you will be the same as for everyone: What is your opinion of Preston Walton?"

Miss Ying thought about the question for a moment. "He could make a suitable bitch," she said nonchalantly. "But his self-control is weak, his attitude coddled, and his tolerance for pain… less than acceptable."

Miss Ying stood up and stepped towards the scales, coin in hand. She dropped it on the devil's side, the small silver platter sinking down, and then returned to her seat in the juror's box.

"Short and sweet. That's always appreciated," said Mistress Midori. "Miss Grace?"

Miss Grace got up, Preston's eyes on her swinging hips. She settled into her seat on the stand with a glossy smile. Her eyes flicker down to Preston and away again.

"He was a sweet puppy," she said. "He pushed himself too in trying to please me. I sense… attachment issues, eventually. Maybe pride issues. But like I said, sweet. I think he would benefit from a strict hand for a while to cement the basics, but I think, like, it'll be frustrating for whoever that is. And him too, haha…"

Miss Grace went to the judge's bench and Preston's heart fell as she put her coin on the devil's scale, weighing it down further.

Was everyone going to vote for him to be punished?

Lady Khan was next. She sat up straight on the stand, looking eminently comfortable there. As she spoke, she addressed Preston directly.

"You did better than I thought you would, to be honest. Based on the results of your assessment I was expecting someone… more entitled. I was pleasantly surprised. I'll be curious to hear what Dong has to say about your pussy licking skills, but you *definitely* needed work there." The mistresses in the juror's box laughed. "But eagerness is a virtue in my book, so I'll give you that."

Lady Khan went over and deposited her coin on the angel's side of the scales with a small metallic *clink!* As she walked past him, she turned and grinned at him with more of that secret "I know something you don't" knowledge.

2-1, against Preston. He had been counting on Miss Grace's favor and, as he looked over the rest of the mistresses, he didn't like his odds. Daddy Dong went next, looking so much more petite and punky than the woman who had preceded her.

"He reminded me why I became a lesbian," she said, playing to the crowd and drawing surprised laughs. "Keep him away from my little oyster, please, or maybe just put a muzzle on him so no one has to deal with his uncoordinated tongue."

Her vote was obvious: devil all the way.

Well, that's that, thought Preston. *No way I'm getting four votes from what's left.*

A question popped into his head. What happened if the scales were balanced at the end of all this?

Princess Yeona went next, waving to Preston on her way up the witness stand stairs. "Loved him," she said. "Super super fun. Caught on quick when things escalated. I wish every Omakase could.be like this one."

If Princess Yeona was reeling from the discipline she'd endured, she didn't show it. She practically bounced up out of her chair to drop her coin on the angel's scale, moving the score to 3-2.

The severe, stern Queen Haewon was next. When she was seated she cleared her throat and said only a single word: "Approved."

Preston watched goggle-eyed as the mistress went over and put her coin on the angel's side, evening out the scales. He couldn't believe it. Maybe he could pull this off after all.

Miss Sayaka took the stand, her lolita stockings swishing seductively as she passed by Preston.

"It was touch and go for a while there," she said. "I really thought he was going to fizzle out and fail, and I was ready to write him off."

Preston's hopes began to soar.

"But Lady Khan was right there's–"

"Let's refrain from talking about that," said Mistress Midori. The two exchanged hushed words in rapid Japanese. Miss Sayaka nodded.

"Well, he passed the bar I had for him," she said. "There's something very interesting there, and I agree with Miss Grace that the right hand can bring it out."

She got up, striding towards the scales with her va-va-voom walk and dropped her coin on the angel's scale. It was 4-3 now, victory just a vote away.

Madam Fei got up on the stand, smoothing out her red silk qipao.

"I'd say stamina's an issue," she said, her voice sounding much more natural and native now. "He barely lasted five minutes. But he's a white guy surrounded by Asian women, so I don't know what I expected."

Snickers spread throughout the juror's box and Mistress Midori shot them a chiding glance.

Madam Fei continued: "His bowing needs work too, though he didn't cry for mercy so he's got that going for him... I guess."

The Chinese mistress stood and, as Preston had already guessed, dropped her coin on the devil's scale. The votes were even, 4-4.

"Well, well, well... we have a tie," said Mistress Midori. "My favorite."

Preston thought she was being sarcastic, but as she smiled broadly, she seemed to actually be serious.

"That leaves the final vote up to me," she continued. "This seems like the right time to ask you, Preston, what you would like to say on your own behalf." She looked at him expectantly.

"From here?" he asked, having somewhere thought in the back of his mind that he would've at least been freed to sit on the witness stand and give his own testimony.

Mistress Midori tweaked her lips to the side. "Or you could not speak at all," she said.

Preston strained his eyes to try to look at the juror's box but he couldn't see it at all. "Uh... what should I say? What am I, um, allowed to say?"

Mistress Midori suppressed a sigh and said: "Why don't you try telling us what you learned here these past 24 hours. Or you could always abstain and I can vote accordingly…"

Preston perked up. "I can say something," he blurted out. "I learned… I…" Everything crashed down on him at once: every single little moment in the Silk Dungeon, every act of humiliation, of degradation, of having something shoved in his face that he wanted, of having to perform, of finding something inside himself he didn't know was there.

Of realizing that his long-standing, deep-seated drive to succeed in life wasn't based on being rich or powerful or privileged. It was, as Mistress Midori had said herself, a mask to cover up the most fragile parts of himself that his jealousy had greedily preyed upon for years and years and years.,.

"I fucked up," said Preston.

The room went silent.

Preston continued: "I wanted something, a long, long time ago. People– women–like you. I wanted to be, you know… with them. Close to them. In their orbit, at the risk of sounding cheesy."

"Just say you wanted to fuck them," said Daddy Dong, the group split between laughing and shooting her annoyed looks.

"But I didn't have that drive the other guys did," Preston pushed on, his face flushed with embarrassment. "I wasn't interested in fucking someone like some animal or being a big man or whatever. But I also wasn't weak. I wanted to be, I dunno, strong but weak? Weak but strong?" Preston took a chance: "Dominated but still of value?"

None of the mistresses said anything.

"I don't know where any of that leaves me now. But I do know something inside me has changed, like finally seeing a pattern in my own behavior and now, with that, I can maybe change the cycle I'm in and do something else. Something that would make me happier. I don't know what that is, but knowing that has got to be worth something… right?

Mistress Midori mulled over Preston's words.

"After listening to that, along with the testimony of the mistresses, I think there's only one clear choice for me to make." She picked up her coin from the shelf of her judge's bench and held it between the scales. "Preston Walton, as acting judge of this trial and Head Mistress of the Silk Dungeon, I declare you guilty and deserving of punishment.

She dropped her coin on the devil's platter, its weight breaking the balance of the scales.

PUSSY WHIPPED

Not more punishment. The fronts of Preston's shins still ached from the bowing ritual Madam Fei had made him perform, his ass and nipples still tender from Queen Haewon's abuse. He couldn't take anymore and raged in his stocks in fear and frustration.

"No! Please, no!" he cried. The metal latch holding the stock together rattled wildly. "Don't punish men! Please!"

Mistress Midori had already stepped down from the judge's bench, her fishnet bodysuit even more sensual now that Preston could see it in full. It was like she was wearing nothing at all, her skin made of fine weave fishnet. She turned her back to him, showing him how the fishnet clung between her buttocks and showed the swell of her breasts from behind, and clicked open a panel built into the front of the judge's bench. It swung open to reveal a war chest of Dungeon toys–paddles, floggers, crops, canes, and many, many more. The mistress took out a thick, single-tail whip and cracked it in the air. It made a terrifying noise.

"I'll do anything," begged Preston. His heart raced madly. "Anything you want, anything at all!"

Mistress Midori tested the whip again, snapping it away from the juror's box.

"It takes a surprising amount of skill and practice to use a whip correctly," she informed Preston. "Even cracking it correctly isn't easy, let alone hitting what you're aiming for. Luckily for you, I'm an expert."

"Please…" Preston's voice became whiny and afraid. "I'm begging you, Mistress. Have mercy…"

"This *is* merciful," said Mistress Midori. She walked over to Preston, body bouncing in her fishnet stocking. She wiped the start of a tear off his face. "Punishment is a gift. It cleanses and clarifies, makes one stronger."

The mistress held the butt of the whip out from between her thighs, pushing it out towards Preston like a cock. He saw the handle was leather-wrapped steel with the initials "MM" on the base.

"Show me you're grateful for the gift I am going to give you and kiss my whip," said Mistress Midori.

Preston's glassy eyes stared up at her, still hoping she would change her mind. Her expression was unyielding. With trembling lips, Preston kissed the butt of the whip, letting his mouth linger on it for a moment. Then he closed his eyes and hung his head and, as he accepted what was going to happen, a rush of adrenaline ran through his body, making him start to shake uncontrollably. He sniffled. This was really going to happen–he was going to be whipped in front of all these women. Mistress Midori gently petted his head.

"Deep breaths," she told him. "You will get through this."

Once she stepped behind him, Preston's pulse really started to race. Her hand touched his back and he jumped in the stocks. She drew her hand down to his ass and rubbed her palm against his cheeks, warming them. Then with both hands she tore the open crotch of his prison uniform pants a little bit wider, either to give herself a bigger target or to keep the thin, rough fabric from getting in the way. When she was done making her minute adjustments, she held her palm to his back again to feel the rise and fall of his frenzied breathing.

"Preston Walton. You shall receive three lashes as punishment. With each lash, I on behalf of the Silk Dungeon urge you to consider how you might embrace what you see as weakness and take that into the core of yourself. While these lashes will hurt, they will also strengthen you through the act of submission to my whip. And a final word of advice before we begin: do not fight your pain. Give into it."

Mistress Midori lifted her hand and Preston waited. In a sense, he was grateful to be so thoroughly bound in the stocks, unable to move his arms or feet. It meant there was no choice to make–no running, no shielding himself–just acceptance. He took long, loud, heavy breaths.

Pain. Blistering, slicing, mind-obliterating pain, set to the deafening fireworks crack of the whip. Preston screamed as loud as he could, so loud he could feel it strain his vocal cords, and whatever concentration he'd built up was instantly broken as he thrashed in the stocks. He immediately began to sob.

"One," counted Mistress Midori. She tested the whip in the air above Preston several times, each roaring snap making him cower and cry in fear. His legs shook and his ass felt like it had been set on fire.

The whip landed again, and this time Preston was acutely aware of how it slashed down the pillow of one cheek. In his mind, he saw a knife slicing open a couch cushion and he blubbered out another scream as he pushed himself into the stocks in a feverish attempt to escape the pain. He flailed, body fighting the heavy wood beams of the stocks, the metal latch jangling angrily.

"Aaaarrggghhh, no, no no NO!" he yelled, feeling a trickle down his thigh that might as easily be sweat or blood. He choked on his tears. "N-n-nooo, I cc-c-can't take anymore, I can't!"

"Two," said Mistress Midori, slowly enunciating the word. "There will be no concessions. You will take the punishment I give you. Now breathe and prepare yourself."

Preston gasped wetly, filling his lungs as much as his wound-tight body would allow. He drew long inhalations in through his nose and let them out in quick, successive puffs like he was going through labor. Time seemed to slow down, threatening–promising–to stop. Preston stared straight ahead at the now empty judge's bench and witness stand, taking a mental snapshot of the moment.

When the last lash fell, something in Preston broke. It wasn't tears or fear or panic. It was something more deep-set than that, something foundational, like the body-shattering strike of the whip had revealed a fatal flaw in his own construction, causing him to crumble. He didn't scream this time, He simply took the pain in all its raging fury, whatever fight left in his body fading away to leave him slumped in the stocks; had he not been supported by the ankle cuffs and the wooden beams, Preston was sure he would've collapsed to the floor.

"Three," Mistress Midori said. She came back around in front of Preston and held the butt of the whip to his mouth again. He didn't need to be told to kiss it this time, placing his lips on its tip obediently, almost adoringly. The mistress stroked his hair. "There's one other thing for you to receive."

Preston's head dropped, ready to accept whatever further punishment the mistress had in store for him.

"A new name," she said, smiling softly at Preston as he looked up at her. "I and the other mistresses had a heated debate on what we thought would be the most appropriate name for you and we've decided to name you: Kuchi."

"Coochie?" asked Preston.

Mistress Midori was ready with a smirk. "Kuchi. It's Japanese and it can mean mouth or orifice or entrance or vacancy. And yes, it does have a particular sound in English, doesn't it? It suits you well."

The mistress went back to the hidden cabinet and put the single-tail whip back. She took out a fat black marker from a basket on the cabinet's upper shelf, uncapping it as she returned to Preston.

"Would you like me to write your new name on your forehead so everyone will remember?" she asked.

Preston nodded. "Yes... Mistress," he said.

In big Japanese characters, Mistress Midori wrote Kuchi on Preston's forehead. She nodded approvingly at her handiwork before addressing the other women: "Mistresses, can you help me clean up Kuchi here and prepare the rest of the festivities?"

Preston heard the women rise from the juror's box, low conversation breaking out amongst them. They seemed to split into two or three groups, one coming up behind Preston to apply a soothing balm to his tortured backside. A rich, herbal smell wafted towards him. Mistress Midori crouched down to face Preston directly.

"You did very, very well," she said to him. "I'm proud of you. And I need you to know you had to be punished—not to hurt you, but to help you heal. You might not understand it now, but you will in time."

But the thing was, Preston did understand—at least a little bit, anyway. Something about the pain of the punishment had left him changed, like he'd shed an old skin and emerged new, ready for life in an all-new way. Mistress Midori traced her fingers around Preston's lips as the mistresses being him applied bandages to his buttocks that must've had some kind anesthetic on them that helped numb the fiery ache across his cheeks.

When Preston had been bandaged up, the mistresses cut away his cheap prison uniform with pairs of safety scissors. Mistress Midori unlatched the wooden stocks and released the snap cuffs around his ankles, all of the mistresses around him carefully lowering Preston to the floor in front of Mistress Midori's fishnet-covered feet. She wiggled her toes at him.

"Show me that kuchi, Kuchi," said Mistress Midori.

Commanded by his new submissive name, Preston kissed Mistress Midori's toes and the tops of her feet, lavishing attention on the woman who had just whipped him into an incoherent state. By the logic of the outside world, such a show of reverence should've been unthinkable, but Preston savored every single kiss, feeling deeply safe under the mistress's gaze.

"That's enough," Mistress Midori said.

Preston had to pull his lips away, looking sad that his time worshiping the mistress's feet was already at an end.

"Don't worry," she said. "We're not done with you yet."

Hands reached under Preston's armpits, bringing him to his feet. It was Miss Grace and Miss Ying and together they helped Preston follow after Mistress Midori, going slow to make sure he didn't stumble. They went behind the judge's bench, where the other mistresses had quickly set up a perverse scene: a raised, bench-like table clearly intended for Preston, with a padded headrest on one side and an indent on the other for someone to stand directly behind him, between his legs. Miss Grace and Miss Ying guided him onto the table and strapped him in, neck, wrists, legs, and ankles all. Preston watched as Miss Sayaka handed out strap-on harnesses to the other mistresses, a few putting them on immediately, others waiting and holding them by their sides instead.

Miss Grace stepped in front of Preston, pressing a button underneath the bench-like table to lower Preston's face until he was staring at her crotch. She started to undo her pants. She'd exchanged her pink ruffle thong for a black satin one that carried the dizzying scent of her pussy.

"You've been waiting so patiently for this," she said to him as she pulled the thong down, revealing her slit. "Now it's all yours."

As Preston began to lick Miss Grace's lips, he felt the familiar cool drizzle of lube between his ass cheeks. Gloved hands stroked his hips.

"Open up for me, puppy," said Miss Ying, pushing a slicked dildo into Preston's ass.

Preston tongued Miss Grace's pussy while he was fucked from behind, his own cock growing from the twin sensations. Music filled the room, sultry, trip-hoppy R&B that set the mood as the mistresses laughed and chatted and sipped on champagne handed to them by two female waiters, including the one Preston had spoken to earlier.

For the next hour, Preston ate pussy and took cock, used like some kind of party favor by the Asian women as they got more and more tipsy from champagne. Some of the mistresses who fucked him didn't bother to announce themselves, adding to Preston's humiliation, while other mistresses came by for extra helpings of Preston's "kuchi", with Princess Yeona even giving him a sip of champagne before he ate her out for the third time. No pussy was left unlicked–even Daddy Dong made use of Preston's mouth, critiquing his technique and giving him even more instruction on how to nipple at the labia, tongue the taint, and gently suck the clit.

When Preston was ordered to pleasure Mistress Midori through her fishnet, Madam Fei and Miss Sayaka flanked Preston on either side, Miss Sayaka playing with his tender nipples and Madam Fei stroking Preston's cock, backing off whenever he got close to cumming; he didn't know who was fucking him this time, but based on the harsh thrusting, he guessed it was Queen Haewon. Mistress Midori held Preston's head in her hands as he serviced her. His tongue grew heavy and raw from the sopping wet weave of the head-to-toe stocking.

"He's definitely upped his body count after this weekend," Miss Ying quipped as she watched the show. "What's it now? Twelve? Thirteen?"

Mistress Midori hmmed. "We can pump those numbers up if you want, Kuchi," she said to Preston between breathy sighs. "We could have two dozen twenty-something girls ready to fuck you in the ass within the hour. Just say the word."

The women laughed and whoever was drilling Preston's ass slapped his cheek, right next to one of the numbing whip bandages. It definitely had to be Queen Haewon, thought Preston.

As the party quieted, mistresses bid Preston farewell, allowing him to kiss their hands and boots and asses to show his respect. After planting a kiss on the top of Lady Khan's hand, she bent down to speak directly to him.

"I'm sorry," she said.

Preston raised his eyebrows, tongue too tired to even think of asking her why.

"What I said about isolating the intelligence part of your assessment… I made that up," admitted Lady Khan. "The rest of the insights were true, but to be perfectly honest with you, you're quite intelligent according to the questions you answered."

Preston blinked. Was she serious?

Lady Khan stroked his cheek. "But consider this: You were ready to believe me. That doesn't make you less intelligent, but it does suggest something else–something about you being ready to be told what to think. See you next time, Tiger."

That left just Preston and Mistress Midori. She unfastened his bindings and said nothing as she led him away. Preston didn't ask where they were going–didn't think to ask Mistress Midori anything anymore, just to obey–and was unsurprised when they rode up the main elevator back to the 11th floor. They went to her room. Preston's clothing was there, folded up all nice and neat on the table. He was strangely sad to see that.

"Our time is almost up," she said. "Was this the kind of adventure you were looking for?"

"Yes," croaked Preston, mouth still flooded with the scent of pussy. "I… I know this should be the make-believe and the world outside real, but after this past day, I'm not entirely sure which is which anymore."

Mistress Midori quietly laughed to herself. "That happens," she said.

Looking down at his feet, Preston couldn't bring himself to laugh with her. He would soon be going home to his beautiful, empty, sterile apartment and then, come Monday morning, back to work to give orders and hold meetings with casual millionaires and industry thought leaders. The thought of it made him nauseous.

"Go in the corner and face the wall, Kuchi," said Mistress Midori in a commanding voice.

Delighted to be ordered around, Preston padded to the corner of the room and got down on his knees. Mistress Midori came up behind him and pushed his nose so that it was touching the corner itself, setting a bundled up tissue on the bridge of his nose.

"Don't you dare let that drop," she warned. "I need to feel a cock in me and that's something you're not allowed to watch."

He heard one of the nightstand drawers open and listened as the room was slowly filled with the sounds of Mistress Midori's deep, erotic moaning. Preston's cock poked into the corner and he desperately wanted to stroke himself off to the sounds of the Japanese mistress's self-pleasure.

But he wouldn't dare touch himself without permission and had never been so happy to not get something he wanted.

EPILOGUE: 3 MONTHS LATER

Mistress Midori popped the piece of yellowtail in her mouth, chewing with satisfaction as Preston spoke. They were sitting at Akikos on Folsom Street for lunch, the mistress in a subdued women's business suit and Preston in a puffy Patagonia vest and khakis.

"My sabbatical starts next week," said Preston. "It's set for an entire year but I don't know…. I might not go back."

"You'll have plenty of time to figure that out," said Mistress Midori. She refilled Preston's sake. "There's not exactly a lot to do on Danshu Island after lights out. At least not for where you'll be staying."

"Yeah, I get that impression," said Preston. The server placed a fresh piece of fish in front of them, which they both quickly enjoyed. He and the mistress locked eyes and shared a smile. "Isn't this where you ask me if I'm sure about this?"

"I think I'd prefer to wait until I visit you there," said Mistress Midori. She leaned across the table and whispered to Preston. "It will be *so* much more fun to ask you if you think you've made a mistake when you're already a few weeks into being treated like a prisoner by the women on Danshu. Assuming you haven't lost your speaking privileges by then. I hear it's very common for American men who go there."

Preston chuckled nervously.

"I heard they shave your head and give you a temporary tattoo on your scalp when you arrive," he said, fishing for information. "Is that true?"

Mistress Midori shrugged. "Different 'visitors' receive different experiences. I'm sure they'll figure it out with you before you get there. It's the system Lady Khan was inspired by, after all. But one thing is for certain—you will never feel more controlled in your life. I recommend you savor the simple pleasures of life before you lose them. Speaking of…"

The mistress opened up an app on her phone and tapped a button. Preston felt a shock between his legs, his chastity cage burning with electricity for one hot second. His leg bumped the table and the diners around them turned to look at what the noise was.

When they went back to minding their own business, Mistress Midori said: "I have a dildo-gag and a blindfold waiting for you in my chambers. I thought about shocking you every three minutes until we get up there but I'm only going to set the timer for every five. Isn't that kind of me?"

"Yes, Mistress," Preston said. "Thank you, Mistress."

"You're very, very welcome, Kuchi."

Preston ached in his cage as he waited for the next shock.

THE END

MICHELLE LUCIA WANTS TO SAY...

Thanks for reading! I hope you enjoyed the story. Want another story, 100% FREE? I'll make you a deal: if you sign up for my newsletter today, I'll send you an exclusive download link to my Tease & Denial Femdom Erotica Chastity Checkup! It's the story of a boyfriend put in his place by his domineering girlfriend--at the dinner table in front of her college bestie! It's filled with delicious humiliation and nasty surprises.

This 6,400-word ebook is no longer available anywhere on Amazon, so sign up today and grab your exclusive free copy! I promise your information won't be shared with anyone else and that I'll keep you in the know on my new releases, special offers, and calls for advance readers.

https://mlpaige.link/mailinglist

All you've got to do is open the link and follow the instructions. Thanks again! Stay kinky, ~ Michelle Lucia

KINK APPENDIX

A list of kinks and fetishes in A Night at the Silk Dungeon (those denoted by an asterisk are more likely to seen as intense):

Anal Plugs
Analingus/Rimming, Mild
Asian Cultural Roleplay
Asian Women (18+)
Bondage, Armbinders
Bondage, Bodybag
Bondage, Gags
Bondage, Hoods
Bondage, Leg Restraints
* Bondage, Nose Hook
Bondage, Stocks
CBT, Ball Spanking
CBT, Light Toe Kicking
CBT, Mild Electricity
CEI, Self
Chastity, Male & Female
Cunnilingus, Actual
Cunnlingus, Simulated
Dehumanization, Mild
Discipline, General
Electricity Simtulation
Emasculation, Mild
* Enema Play, Discomfort (Minimal Physical Detail)
Exhibitionism, All Parties Consenting and 18+
Facesitting
Female-on-female Domination
* Foodplay, Mouth-to-plate feeding (Minimal Physical Detail)
Foot Worship
Group Humilaition, 18+ Female Audience
Human Furniture, Ashtray (Gag)Human Furniture, Footstool

Human Furniture, Table
Humiliation
Impact Play, Caning
Impact Play, Cropping
Impact Play, General
Impact Play, Hairbrush
Impact Play, Hand
* *Impact Play, Whipping (Medium-Hard, Minimal Physical Detail)*
Interrogation Roleplay, Mild
Material, Lace
Material, Latex
Material, Leather
Mental Domination
Namecalling, in Roleplays
Nipple Torture, Medium
Objectification, Mild
Office Ladies
Orgasm Control
Orgasm Denial
Panties, Gag
Panties, Sniffing
PIV Sex, in Bondage (Consensual)
PIV Sex, Simulated with Strap-on
Predicament Play
Prisoner / Prison Guard Roleplay, Mild
Professional Dominatrix
Prostate Orgasm
Prostate Stimulation
Puppy Play
Ritual Discipline, Kneeling with Pain
Royalty Roleplay
Scent Play, Intimate Body Parts
Sensory Deprivation
Spanking, Barehanded
Spanking, Hairbrush
Spit Play, Mild
Strap-on, Pegging
Strap-on, Simulated Fellatio

Sweat Licking
Tease & Denial
* Toilet Humilaition, Non-visual Witnessing
Training, Protocol
Training, Puppy
Uniforms
Verbal Humiliation, in Roleplays

Printed in Great Britain
by Amazon